HIDALGO'S BEARD

HIDALGO'S BEARD

BEARD

A CALIFORNIA FANTASY
by
Conger Beasley, Jr.

SANTA FE

Sunstone books may be purchased for educational, business, or sales promotional use.
For information please write: Special Markets Department, Sunstone Press,
P.O. Box 2321, Santa Fe, New Mexico 87504-2321.

Printed on acid-free paper

Library of Congress Cataloging-in-Publication Data

Beasley, Conger.
  Hidalgo's Beard : a California Fantasy / by Conger Beasley, Jr.
    pages cm
  ISBN 978-0-86534-953-7 (softcover : alk. paper)
  1. Life change events--Fiction. I. Title.
  PS3552.E175H53 2013
  813'.54--dc23

                            2013018882

WWW.SUNSTONEPRESS.COM
SUNSTONE PRESS / POST OFFICE BOX 2321 / SANTA FE, NM 87504-2321 /USA
(505) 988-4418 / ORDERS ONLY (800) 243-5644 / FAX (505) 988-1025

For
John and Doris Little

Man cannot achieve knowledge
Except what water yields to mortal mind

Edward Dahlberg

CHAPTER I

1.

Someone was calling my name. "Navvy . . . Navvy . . . wake up!" I was awake. I'd been awake for a long time, staring up at the surface, the crumpled reflection of the palm trees floating on top of the water. "Come out of there, Navvy, right now!"

I rolled over, releasing a cloud of bubbles that spiraled up to the surface. Judging from the glare, it was probably mid-afternoon. Up there, out of the water, it was hot, 115 degrees or more, cruel and merciless.

"Come up here, Navvy, right now! We're expected at Andrea's at 5:30 and I don't want to be late!" He was standing on the end of the diving board, leaning over, staring into the deep end. "I got the key from Mrs. Baines, and if you don't come out she's given me permission to drain the pool. Do you hear?"

All week he'd been threatening to do that. From the drain, his face looked bloated and swollen, the features streaked like a watercolor painted by an amateur. There was something menacing about the face, yet removed from it by twelve feet of chlorinated water I couldn't get too upset. It was merely my father with another silly request.

"I don't want to go to Andrea's!" I shouted through a rush of bubbles. "I want to stay right here!"

"I'll give you ten minutes, and if you're not out by then I'm going to drain the pool. Mrs. Baines has given me full permission to do whatever's necessary to make you cooperate. Are you listening? You have exactly ten minutes to get out of the pool and into the house!"

His voice was harsh. No doubt he would drain the pool if I didn't come out. Ever since I entered the water a week ago he'd been furious, coming down in the mornings, cursing and calling me names.

I thrashed my heels against the drain. Naturally, my father wanted me to meet the woman he intended to marry. Twice in the last week he'd brought her down to the pool to introduce her. Looking up from the drain, I saw a pale, lumpy face topped with a clump of tinted hair. Her eyes were underscored with heavy marks which masked her face but not the look of repugnance that crept across her mouth as she gazed into the water.

I blew her a kiss and rolled over.

2.

After drying off I looked for something to wear. A week in the water had swollen my body considerably. My skin was hard and rubbery and was beginning to turn green. The lids of my bulging eyes secreted a mucus which enabled me to keep them open underwater for long periods of time. My feet were flat, the toes melding together to give me a strong kick. My hair, normally curly, was plastered to my scalp in a sleek cap. Gills slashed my throat. This development was most promising; already I could remain submerged for several hours without surfacing.

In the mirror my chest bulged like a barrel, though my arms and legs had each shrunk several inches. I could barely button my shirt; the sleeves drooped over my fingers, so I rolled them up to my elbows. The cuffs of my blue slacks were too long and had to be folded up and pinned to the crease. Walking was a chore—my feet, with the toes pressed together, were like stumps, and it was hard to maintain balance. I wanted to lie down, stretch out, get level. My once-thin face ballooned like a medicine ball. My mouth was a gash, and my teeth had partially receded into my gums. What neck I had disappeared into my shoulders. To offset the fishy odor that wafted off my body, I dabbed a little cologne under each ear and waddled into the living room where my father sat reading the Los Angeles *Times*.

"How do I look?" I said casually.

3.

"You can't be serious about this," he said as we drove into Palm Springs.

"I am."

"It's ridiculous. You're making a dumb mistake."

"I see it differently."

My body felt like it was coated with wax. An hour out of the water and already my skin was starting to itch.

"You can't expect to live down there!" he exploded.

"Why not?"

"Because . . . because it's just not done. People don't live at the bottom of swimming pools."

"I'm going to."

"Dammit, Navvy, I didn't send you to those fancy

3

schools to have you end up like this!"

"No, Pop, you sent me to those fancy schools to obtain the education you were never able to obtain for yourself. You sent me to those fancy schools to round out a part of yourself that was denied the same opportunity by circumstances beyond your control. And believe me, I'm grateful. I had a good time, and I learned a lot."

"The hell you did!"

"Watch out for that car!" I was having trouble with my eyes; everything looked fuzzy.

"Why, Navvy?" His voice cracked. "I thought you liked working in the library. I thought you were finally settling down."

"I am settling down, Pop. *Straight* down."

He fumbled for a cigarette. I pushed in the dash lighter and held it up in my clumsy fingers.

"I'm embarrassed," he muttered through a cloud of smoke. "Andrea's embarrassed. Everybody at the club is embarrassed."

"I'm sorry. When I finally get adjusted I'll move. I promise."

"Where to?"

"Lake Cahuilla. Maybe the Salton Sea."

"You wouldn't last a day in that water."

"I don't know; I'm getting tougher. Maybe they'll let me stay at the bottom of the pool at the Spa or the Riviera. As a kind of curiosity, a tourist attraction."

He dragged on the cigarette, considering the possibility. "Nah . . . it's too crazy."

"It's so restful, Pop. I wish you'd understand that."

"You're not supposed to rest in life," he growled. "You're supposed to work."

"I know . . . I know."

4

"Well? That's something you've done precious little of in your life."

"I'm not going to argue with you," I said wearily. "I've had jobs, I've worked before."

"Sure... sure."

"Work like that doesn't do anything for me, Pop."

He stared at me till the tires bumped against the curb. Then he wrenched the wheel over and steered the car back onto the road. "It makes you a living! What the hell's wrong with making a living!"

"I don't care much about making a living."

"Wonderful... wonderful! What if the president didn't care much about politics?"

"In the water I don't eat much. I don't have to wear anything. Best of all, I can hear all sorts of fantastic things."

"Please... please."

"I can, Pop. I hear the strangest things. I hear people in other pools. I hear fish in the Salton Sea. I hear hawks high up in the mountains..."

"Navvy, for Christ's sakes!"

"Come down with me sometime! You could rent a scuba tank and we could spend the whole day together!"

"I need a drink... a tall, stiff drink."

4.

Andrea greeted us at the door. "Hello, Brad," she grinned, giving my father a kiss. "And Navvy, at long last! How nice to meet you!"

She squeezed my puffy hand. Highlighted by an adroit use of make-up, the ruin of her handsome face

5

stood out through a screen of bags and folds. Scrolls of loose flesh dangled off her jaw; the corners of her mouth dissolved into tiny wrinkles. Her eyes looked muddy and soiled, like headlights in a fog. Too much booze, though she was making an effort to cut back. At the bar she mixed vodka martinis for us and splashed a little vermouth on the rocks for herself. "Just to fool myself into thinking it's the real thing," she chuckled.

The living room was already crowded. I stumbled in behind my father, trying to maintain my balance. Around the room we went, greeting people. I only knew one or two; my father knew enough to feel comfortable, but then he always felt comfortable in a roomful of people, whether he knew them or not.

The condominium was located deep inside a guarded compound next to the fairway leading to the seventh green. My father had played golf there and pronounced the course satisfactory. Glass doors, ten feet high, opened onto a patio cluttered with wrought-iron furniture. The doors were partially screened by drapes that filtered out the late afternoon sun. The living room had a definite resort look to it. A combed shag rug, thick enough to lose your toes in, covered the floor. Rattan furniture, cushioned with a tufted chintz pattern, was scattered about in conversational groupings. A coffee table, lacquered black with a tortoise shell band, sat between two large couches decorated with a warp-weave floral print. A crystal chandelier with mirrored prisms dangled from the ceiling over an antique white dining table. On the walls hung a collection of desert scenes by a young Moroccan artist.

The guests were friendly and good-natured, year-round residents of Palm Springs. Women outnumbered the men by half—faded, leathery beauties with streaked hair and cracked skin. Beads and bracelets jangled off their wrists and wrinkled throats; a dozen turquoise rings clinked against a dozen crystal cocktail glasses producing a tintinnabulation over the babble of conversation.

I decided Andrea must be pretty sure of my father to let him loose among these jackals. Sixty-three years old, tan and healthy from playing golf, he was an excellent prospect. Though short in stature, he stood very erect, with broad shoulders and wavy black hair which, only in the last few years, had begun to gray seriously. A bold nose struck off his face, his mouth was wide and handsome, his dark eyes crinkled with good humor. A crowded room invariably brought out the best in him, an unmistakable charm, a sincere desire to please others and make them feel at ease.

"How are you, Navvy?" asked Andrea. "I saw you the other day in the pool but didn't get a chance to say hello."

"Hot . . . dry," I whispered. I purposely kept my voice low to avoid making the clicking sound which invariably filled my throat whenever I tried to say anything out of the water. A deep, resonant click between words that sounded like an elephant hiccuping.

Several women gathered around, snorting and blowing smoke in my face. Delicious old bags with crumbling faces and yellow teeth, they stroked my spongy flesh and fussed over how healthy I looked. One of them, Hetty, a few years older than my father and a good friend of Andrea's, had been a script girl at MGM during the 1930s. "Clark was always on time, never missed a scene, a true professional," she replied, in response to a question from Andrea. "When he came on the set, he had his

7

lines pat and went through rehearsals without a flaw.

"One day Mr. Mayer called me into his office and asked if I had any advice about how to handle Spencer. I was just a lowly script girl then, what did I know about handling a talented but rowdy young film star? But Mr. Mayer was at his wit's end and was asking everyone for advice about what to do with this cantankerous new sensation. We were shooting *Raider's Roost* . . . no, it was *Almaviva's Fever* . . . and Spence was drinking heavily. This was before he met Katie and all *that* began. 'Well, I don't know what to say, Mr. Mayer,' I said. 'Spence is so awfully good, I'd humor his peccadilloes. I do know he's a Catholic, with a great sense of personal honor and pride. I grew up with lots of Catholic boys in St. Louis, and being Catholic myself, or being one back then, I think I know how Catholic boys feel. Why don't you take him to lunch someday, let him drink himself *green* in the face, then during the afternoon shooting when he makes an ass out of himself, he'll feel terribly embarrassed and apologetic and probably will never do it again.'

"Well, there I was, all of twenty years old, never been kissed, let alone really tampered with, giving advice to a lordly movie mogul like Mr. Louis B. Mayer. But do you know, he took my advice and the very next day he went with Spence out to lunch and got him drunk as a skunk. The afternoon shooting was a disaster: Spence flubbed his lines, couldn't remember a cue, and fell all over the set. It was a pitiful sight; I almost burst into tears. But it worked. Spence was so embarrassed he apologized next day to the cast and crew and promised to behave in the future like a gentleman and a professional."

"Navvy . . . excuse me, girls . . . I want Navvy to meet Dr. Bilkstrode. Dr. Bilkstrode, this is my son, Navvy

Dypes."

An enormous man. Six-and-a-half feet tall, with pudgy jowls, plump fingers, and a waist as round as a cistern. His pale gray eyes skidded over my face like ice cubes.

"I want Dr. Bilkstrode to look at you."

"There's nothing wrong with Navvy," Hetty declared. "Leave him alone."

My father shot her a nasty look. "Doc," he said, "my son spent all last week at the bottom of a swimming pool. I know people do weird things out here, but that isn't normal. Look at his skin. Look at his face."

"Ahh-hummm." The doctor's voice was deep and ominous. "And how did you find your . . . swim, young man?"

"Very refreshing. How about a drink?"

"Let the doc look at you first. Look at him, doc."

"I'll get you a drink," said Hetty.

"Look at his skin!" my father exclaimed. "It's green. Wouldn't you call that green, doc?"

"I certainly would. May I have your wrist, please?"

"Let go of my wrist."

"Navvy, he wants to find out what's wrong with you."

"There's nothing wrong with me!"

"I think he looks fine," said Hetty, back with the drink. "Mind your own business, Brad."

My father muttered something under his breath.

"Does he want an injection?" said Dr. Bilkstrode. "I can give him an injection. I have my case in the car."

"I don't want an injection!"

"Hell, doc, I don't know. It's more like he needs his head examined."

"Does he need a psychiatrist? I know a competent

psychiatrist."

"He needs someone to pry open his skull and look inside with a strong light."

I downed the vodka in one gulp.

"I have my stethoscope in the car. I can take his pulse and listen to his chest."

"I don't want my pulse taken!"

"Let me get you another drink," said Hetty.

"Hardening of the epidermal tissues is a frequent complaint in the desert," said Dr. Bilkstrode.

"I've heard of it before," said Andrea. "There's a lady in Rancho Mirage—"

"However, with proper therapy, it can be remedied."

"Give him an injection," said Brad.

"I don't want an injection! Keep your hands off me!"

"Attaboy!" Hetty shouted.

"It may very well be the product of acute anxiety," said Dr. Bilkstrode. "There's a lot of that going around."

"What's he got to be anxious about?" said Brad. "He doesn't even have a job!"

"I've heard," said Andrea, "that when the nerves get overtaxed they harden. It happened to me after my last divorce. For weeks you could bounce a golf ball off my shoulders and hit the ceiling. I didn't turn green though."

"He's sick in the head," Brad insisted.

"Leave me alone!"

"Well, if it's just his skin, we can take care of that," Hetty said, turning to the others. "Can't we girls?"

"You bet!"

"Hetty, please, this is serious."

"I *know* it's serious, Brad. Navvy is having a difficult time readjusting to life on the surface. His skin's tense.

10

We know what to do."

"Be gentle with him!" Andrea called as they led me into the bathroom. A rug with a pile thick as a kelp bed caught my heels. The walls were lined with mirrored panels, illuminated by rows of theatrical lights. Arrangements of pussy willows and eucalyptus decorated the bidet and sink. Cooing like pigeons, the women peeled off my clothes and tossed them in the corner. Then they steered me down into a sunken tub and turned on the gold-plated tap. With their sleeves rolled up, they knelt at the edge of the tub. On a ledge beneath the spigot were cut-crystal decanters filled with buttermilk. They emptied them into the tub and began massaging my parched flesh. The effect was pure ecstasy! As the water rose over my face, my respiration returned to normal, and I felt my muscles unlock, and the tension ease from my body.

5.

"A lot of good those old hags did you," Brad grumbled on the way home. "Your skin's still green and you still have those awful slits on your throat."

"They were nice," I murmured.

"Drunk old bitches."

"They made me feel good."

"Look, Navvy, you can't judge everything in life according to whether it feels good or not. You've got to balance pleasure with pain. You know . . . the old Greek principle. Hell, you know what I mean . . . you had enough education."

11

"It's not just pleasure I'm after, Pop."

"What is it then?"

"Perception ... awareness."

"What the hell does that mean?"

"It's really simple, Pop. There's no special magic to it. You just get into the water and sink down. The deeper you sink the more receptive you become. You discover you're a bundle of highly sensitive nerves and tissues the same as any other organism, and that, when divested of the inhibiting presence of your ego, your body emits a sound frequency that blends perfectly with all the other sounds of the universe."

"That's the dumbest thing I ever heard."

I stared out at the lights of Cathedral City skimming past the car window.

"Ever since your mother died you've acted peculiar. I know her death upset you, but that was five years ago, and we have to go on living. But you've stopped dead in your tracks, Navvy. You dropped out of graduate school when all you had left to do on your Ph.D. was your dissertation. Since then you haven't been able to hold a job. You couldn't even keep the library job I got you in Palm Springs, and that's the easiest job in the world!"

"I want to spend the rest of my life as a fish."

"Well, by God, you can't live with me and be a fish!" he snapped. "You're twenty-seven years old, and you're too old to be a fish!"

Already I could feel the water in the pool, the soothing cushion of the drain.

"I've made an appointment for you to see Dr. Bilkstrode."

A greasy tentacle wormed through my bowels.

"He's expressed an interest in your case. He thinks he

12

can help you."

"He's a roach."

"He is a well-known, highly respected doctor here in the desert, and he wants to help you."

"I don't want to be helped."

"Well, you're going to be, whether you want it or not. I didn't raise you to have you end up at the bottom of a pool. If you won't do this for me, Navvy, then think of your mother. Think of her."

"I do," I said unhappily. "I think of her all the time."

6.

Dr. Bilkstrode's office was in downtown Palm Springs on Palm Canyon Drive. The appointment was for the next afternoon at 3:30. After a restless night in the pool, I emerged around ten, showered, and got dressed.

My father insisted on going with me. I felt like a prisoner, handcuffed to the wrist. In the waiting room he sat reading a magazine and sneaking looks at me. When I excused myself to go to the restroom, he went too.

After twenty minutes, we were ushered into an examination room. I was told to disrobe and put on a white smock. My trousers got caught on my swollen feet and my father had to pull them off. A male nurse with DENNIS embossed on a nameplate weighed me, took my pulse, measured my height, and drew blood from my arm. When he asked if I could piss in a cup, I smiled bleakly and nodded my head. "The doctor will be with you in a few minutes," he said.

The walls of the examination room were covered with grass-patterned paper. Glossy photos of Hollywood personalities like Fatty Arbuckle, Frances Farmer, Lupe Velez, Johnny Stompanato, Theda Bara, Carole Landis, and Ramon Navarro hung everywhere. Ceiling lamps gave off a dazzling glow that magnified the tiny red veins in my father's cheeks. The examination table resembled a sacrificial altar—a solid block of mahogany draped with a burgundy cloth that swept to the floor. A pointed head-rest in the shape of a conquistador's helmet jutted out from one end. Inside were earphones; a control box offered a wide selection of soothing music. A slatted visor could be pulled down over the face to screen out the light. In the corner opposite sat a shiny, chrome desk with fragile legs and drawers the size of laundry hampers. A variety of cacti poked out from a pair of matching bedpans; the desk was littered with crumpled prescription notes and splintered tongue depressors.

Followed by Dennis, Dr. Bilkstrode trundled toward the examination table like an ocean liner toward a pier. Opaque lenses, perched on the bridge of his nose, magnified his eyeballs so they resembled gallstones floating in a dish of bile. I climbed onto the table and put my head inside the conquistador's helmet. Bilkstrode's fingers were the size of kosher hot dogs, but his touch was surprisingly soft. Starting with the vents on my neck, he worked his way down my glistening stomach, poking and prodding. His bushy nostril hair rippled with every exhalation. *"Rayleen trive abstroh menutto,"* he muttered to Dennis, who noted the observation on a pad. Working the stethoscope between my thighs, he placed the cold tip against my scrotum: *"Entrent tris mebbledeen bedarch."*

At the chrome desk, with Dennis clutching his elbow, he lowered himself into a chair. After jotting a few notes, he looked up. This much effort made his face glisten like

14

an empty popcorn bowl. "Well then, young man," he began, "my preliminary diagnosis is that you are suffering from a rampant hormone imbalance which is causing your skin to harden and your eyes to gape. It's located mainly in the Evtuffel gland, though your thyroid is probably involved as well. A phenomenon that is becoming more and more common today. However, it usually affects older people twice your age. Last month I treated a lady with the same malady, only she was sixty-seven. We've had reports of numerous cases up in Orange County and several in San Diego."

"What's the Evtuffel gland, doc?" said Brad.

"A small gland located at the base of the larynx," he said. "A vestigial gland, really. It is believed to be a holdover from the Pleistocene epoch when, due to climatic conditions, man developed a need for a tougher skin. With the rise of civilizations like the Sumerians and Babylonians and man's migration into communal societies where food and shelter were available, this need diminished, and the gland ceased functioning. Periodically, over the past few millenia, it has flared up. The last, most noticeable time was during World War I. The crowded conditions of trench warfare, the squalor in which the soldiers lived, and the tremendous anxiety and fear they suffered reactivated the gland. An Austrian doctor named Frantz Evtuffel treated a number of cases on the Western front between 1915 and 1917 in which the primary symptom was an unusual hardening of the epidermal tissues. With the poisoning of our atmosphere and the overpopulation of our cities, the hardening has reappeared. Mainly, it is a reactive or protective phenomenon, occasioned by a deep, instinctive need on the part of the individual to erect a barrier between himself or herself and the world. In some cases, the barrier is leathery like that of a pachyderm; in others, it is blubbery like a sea lion. You son's seems to be more like a fish, a sort of hybrid between a fish and a seal. The sluices developing on his throat are a most interesting feature. With proper treatment, however, they can be eliminated."

Brad nodded solemnly. My toes turned to ice.

"I'd like him to go into the hospital so we can run more tests. Depending on our findings, it may be necessary to administer a special cure. We need to determine the extent to which the Evtuffel gland is influencing this radical change in his physiognomy. In some individuals, the Evtuffel gland is more volatile than others. The least bit of hypertension will cause it to secrete harmful hormones. Your son might be one of those individuals."

"There's nothing wrong with me," I whispered. How could I make him understand that this was the way I wanted to be? That my condition was the result of an acute case of self-will?

"Of course, my boy. But then all my patients feel that way. Why don't you come around to Eisenhower Medical Center Monday noon? We'll begin testing Tuesday morning. Dennis will make all the appointments and give you the details. If you'd like a private room, I'm sure that can be arranged."

My father clapped his knee. "Hey, Doc, that sounds great! We're on the right track now!"

CHAPTER II

1.

A voice chattering like a magpie woke me up. I rolled over, dragging my elbow across the drain, and bobbed up to a sitting position. "... I envy you... you don't know how lucky you are. Years ago I wanted to do the same thing... but Lake Michigan is a cold place... so I had to stay on top and take my licks like everybody else...."

It was Leo, crazy Leo, who lived in number 14, a few doors from my father's house. What was he doing out in the middle of the night?

"Don't get me wrong, Navvy, I'm not calling you an escapist or anything... I don't know what to call you. You're probably pretty brave... it takes a lot of *chutzpah* to do what you're doing. You've found a place where no one can reach you... like living in a shack in the mountains with no telephone. In the garment industry I couldn't afford not to have a phone. Least not at my shop. In flush times, I was on the phone all day taking orders. But what the hell was I in business for if I didn't want to take orders? Orders is business is business is money. That's what I was in the business for, wasn't it? And to get orders you got to deal with people, lots and lots and lots of people. So what am I kicking about? Most of them was very nice. They made me a good living. They

17

got me to retire out here in the desert, didn't they? So I could play golf every morning and swim in a nice pool?"

A runty fellow wearing a fisherman's hat with a Chicago Bears logo stitched above the bill. Crazy Leo. Cranky, dyspeptic, grumbly Leo, with a mordant wit and a taste for diet lemonade. Wearing, at all hours, around the pool or downtown, frayed and tattered bermuda shorts and rubber-thonged sandals, chewing gum and gesturing with his thumbs at imaginary eavesdroppers lurking behind his back. In his early seventies, his physique was trim, his waist narrow, which was why he never wore a shirt unless a restaurant manager forced him to and certainly never out in the blazing sun. "Jews and lizards don't feel the sun," he explained to me one day. "The one has scales to protect him, the other 4,000 years of history." His face looked as though it had been sculpted by a lumberjack. Stiff, angular nose, square eye sockets, ears like gargoyles, cheek bones flat as shingles. And a voice—that voice—that churned through the water like a propeller on an outboard motor.

"... But every time I step into the pool I'm reminded of something, Navvy. You don't bother me, lying there on the bottom. You're polite and friendly; you even wave as I splash by doing my exercises. You don't get in my way. But you remind me of my cousin Alvah who became a rabbi. And that makes me nervous, Navvy. When we were teenagers, instead of being interested in girls or basketball, Alvah was interested in power. He wanted to be a lawyer, a politician, a judge—something connected with power. He was always talking about power. But then, when he was about twenty, he decided he wasn't interested in that kind of power; he decided he was interested in spiritual power, and so he studied to be a

18

rabbi. The type of power he was interested in was the type you couldn't see, but very powerful nonetheless. He renounced all the worldly power he had accumulated up till then and went around the streets of Chicago in a plain gray coat, mumbling and praying. I thought he was crazy. His family thought he was crazy. Alvah had a real sharp mind, Navvy; he could have made it big in business.

"But as time wore on, I came to envy him. He didn't have to deal with people; I did. And even though I was successful at it, I often wished I could have been successful at something that didn't require as much exposure to the public. I don't know why I'm telling you this, Navvy, you're probably not even listening. But if you are, bear with me a little while. You're the only person who has the slightest chance of understanding what I'm saying. My late wife, bless her, claimed I had the knack for making people want the things I made. I was my own best ad man, she said, better than any of the fancy Chicago agencies I paid thousands of dollars to do the same thing for me. And I was good, Navvy. In my heyday, I could sell a pair of pants to a legless veteran. I could have sold you a pair, right there in the water. I bet I could have gotten you to rise up off the drain and swim over here, with the money in your hand. I was that good.

"But all the time I thought there was something missing. I tried to blame it on the fact that I wasn't a very good Jew. Whenever I put on the phylacteries and read the Torah, I went through the motions. There was more to being a good Jew than just making money. I knew that. But what was it? What kind of power was I really interested in? Did I secretly envy my cousin Alvah and his obsession with God? I think what I envied about him,

Navvy, was his anonymity, the fact that he didn't want to be anybody, the fact that he didn't want to be noticed by anybody. He wanted to be invisible, Navvy, like you. He wanted to sink out of sight so no one could ever interrupt what he enjoyed doing best. That, to him, was real power.

"What's it like to sink out of sight, Navvy? Is it like anything at all? Are you able to concentrate better? Are you able to get to yourself better? I bet it's scary. I bet it's scarier than you thought it would be. What about it, Navvy? Are you scared? Why don't you come up here and tell me whether you're scared or not? I'd like to know. I'm your friend. I have a right to know ...."

2.

Families are filled with anomalies and contradictions, and mine is no exception. What seems commonplace behavior as a child alters radically under the scope of age and scrutiny—the unthinking child becomes the socially conscious adult, and inevitable comparisons are made. I had been over this a thousand times before, with no practical results; but at the bottom of the pool during those early days I had a chance to reflect long and hard on those conditions of my upbringing and heredity that might have contributed to my solemn desire to turn myself into something other than an ordinary human being.

Even before moving out to Palm Springs six months ago from Kansas City, I could detect a change: longer and longer periods spent in the bathtub; an awkward, rolling gait accompanied by a stroking arm motion; gnawing my

20

food in voracious bites; a desire to copulate upside down; a tendency to stop anywhere, day or night, and relieve myself.

Water has always fascinated me. Once immersed for any length of time, it is difficult to pry myself loose. The pressure of the fluid on my skin lulls and enchants me. The feeling of weightlessness, of floating randomly like a particle, unhinges my joints and connective mental fibers and opens ellipses into which drift notions of the arcane and the unspeakable. The result is a distension of awareness that intensifies my powers of perception manyfold over the actual circumference of my body or the circumscriptive range of my reasoning faculties. Like successive rings billowing out from the point of a plunked stone, I feel myself pass over new fields and arenas of experience heretofore unacknowledged. The sensation is exhilarating—like Columbus sighting a green mound on the horizon or the Montgolfier brothers leaping free of the shackles of gravity in a hot air balloon.

Two months ago when I entered the water for my nightly swim, I knew the time would come, and soon, when I would be able to stay under for long periods. I could feel my body changing, subtly at first, then with accelerated urgency—my limbs, eyes, lungs altering their shape to enable me to survive in another medium.

A dream the next night provided further clues. Small, robin-sized creatures with shimmering fins swarmed through my hair. I was outdoors in a meadow, lying face down. Buoyed by the creatures, I levitated off the ground and bobbed toward a copse of trees. Passing between the trunks, I had the distinct sensation of popping through a moist, invisible film. Beyond lurked a murky swamp, in the center of which sat a radio receiver of the type ham operators used in the 1940s. A round speaker, big as a washtub, with a soft mesh webbing, emitted a jabbering lisp. A hypnotic melange of bird screels and insect squabbling leaked over that. Swarming under my chest, the airfish lifted me up and nudged my face against the speaker. For the second time in the dream a membrane gave way, and, guided by the airfish, I swam inside the hole.

Who or what is responsible for this transformation? Is it the product of an act of will, or have I been influenced by outside forces? Am I the prototype of a new kind of creature that will populate the globe at a future date? A passive, secretive creature registering impulses and tabulating sensations?

Freudian psychology provides a description of such tendencies, but not an explanation. The investigative method, with its emphasis upon inductive reasoning, by which Freud first formulated his observations, is inadequate here. We are in the primitive world of anthropomorphic identities, where human, animal, and deific figures merge and blend with lightning speed in a constant search for a more *conscious* being. I am obliged to interpret it as a regression (paradoxically) into future potentialities, a condition of being where the mind deliberately subverts the asphyxiating pressure of material reality by configuring new worlds, and entering them.

This phenomenon utterly baffles my father. He can understand organ transplants; he can tolerate personality changes (my mother had plenty of them in the span of a single day); he is sympathetic to mercurial behavior. But he cannot understand a total physical transformation from one state of being to another. That, he can only attribute to witchcraft.

Of witchcraft there was an element in my family. My uncle—my mother's brother—had an uncanny ability to detect objects below the surface of the water. His intuition was so keen he was used by the Kansas City police whenever there was a drowning in a pond or a lake. The police didn't need to send down divers. My uncle simply walked along the bank till he came to the spot. Sometimes, he even raised the victims by calling out their names in a loud voice, like rescuers used to do with cannon in the nineteenth century. But that wasn't very often. Mostly, he just located the spot, pointed with his finger, and nodded. He claimed he could hear the victims' voices under the water, calling. As he got closer, the voices got louder. His accuracy was fantastic. One victim he found in the Missouri River, above Lexington, nine days after the woman jumped off the ASB bridge in downtown Kansas City. Her body had been carried forty miles downstream. My uncle got in a rubber raft and started downriver, followed by a police boat. He bobbed along with the current, scanning the muddy surface, listening. On the morning of the second day, he heard a peculiar warbling at the tip of a sandbar. Poking about in the shallow water, his fingers got entangled in a mass of hair.

He became a local folk hero. Newspapers sent reporters to interview him; *Life* magazine did a piece on him. He never took any money for the interviews; he never said much anyway. He never divulged his technique, though he was asked a thousand times how he did it. He said he didn't know—he just listened carefully, heard the voices, went to the spot, and that was that. My mother used to say that not only did he find the bodies, he found the souls inside the bodies. By raising the

23

bodies he released the souls. That's why they were calling, she said, so someone would raise their bodies and release their souls. The families of the victims were grateful when he located the bodies, since it meant that their deaths could be properly observed. My uncle never took any money for his efforts, only bus fare to the site and food. He usually stayed overnight with the family of the drowned victim.

He died when I was twelve, but I remember him well. Short and slight, with fair skin, black hair, and round, empty eyes like holes in a hunk of cheese. He enjoyed the company of others, though you got the feeling his mind was elsewhere. He never married, though he had several girlfriends, usually older women, who fussed over him unmercifully. When he came to visit us, he slept outside on a cot. He ate all his food out of an Army mess kit, usually with his fingers or the blade of an old butter knife, hunched over on the floor or outside under a tree.

His own death was peculiar. In the Ozark Mountains of southern Missouri, there's a lake that some people think is the home of a huge water serpent of the Loch Ness variety. The creature was first sighted in the 1940s, floating on the surface on a rainy afternoon. Eyewitnesses claimed it was around fifteen feet long, with an arching neck and sleek, viperish head. Additional sightings were made over the next two decades. In 1954, a woman photographed it with a Polaroid camera, but the print was smudged and could have been faked.

An Ozark society sponsored my uncle to come down and look for the creature. Because of the publicity, he was reluctant but decided to try anyway after talking to my mother. She told him that even if he located the creature he didn't have to tell anyone, and that maybe it would communicate something of interest to him. My father said they were both crazy.

For two weeks he paddled around the lake in his rubber raft, listening and staring into the water. The sponsors grew impatient and grumbled that their money might be better spent on sophisticated sonar gear. For awhile, huge crowds in pleasure crafts followed my uncle around the lake. When he requested that no motorboats approach within 500 yards, people lost interest and went away.

One morning he was out in the middle of the lake. A rowboat filled with observers trailed behind. My uncle paddled a few strokes, then lifted the blade out of the water and listened. He did that about twenty times, cocking his head like a robin tracking a worm. Finally, he looked back at them and said something. At first they didn't understand; then they heard him say, "She's here . . . right below me." And with a grin—that's what the people in the rowboat claimed, and none of them had been drinking—he stood up and jackknifed his body over the side of the raft and disappeared into the water. He never came up again, and all the scuba gear and grappling hooks and searchlights in southern Missouri and northern Arkansas couldn't find a sign of his body or any trace of the lake creature.

Every summer we went to California for a few weeks. My father had relatives in Los Angeles, plus a couple of wartime buddies from the air force. We always stayed at a fancy hotel; when my parents played golf or visited friends, they left me at the swimming pool. By the time I was ten I was a good swimmer, totally unafraid of the deep end. For hours I amused myself with my mask and snorkel, diving for coins and rocks. Even back then, I could hold my breath for a long time. I ignored other kids who tried to play with me. Occasionally, they would race me to the bottom and steal my coins, but I was utterly fearless and chased them till they gave them back.

My parents were drunk most of the time, on scotch and gin, served with grinning aplomb by uniformed waiters and waitresses. How happy they were then, absorbed in one another and their friends. Left alone to amuse myself, armed with a mask and snorkel, I felt like the real parent, puttering around the nest, putting things in order, while the children were off having a good time.

Only when my mother got loaded did she ever venture into the water. Otherwise, despite her brother's predilection, she hated swimming. At the Beverly Wilshire in Los Angeles late one afternoon, she got into the pool with me. She and my father had been partying at a club in Santa Monica, and when they returned she decided to go for a swim. Woozy from all the martinis she'd been drinking, she threaded her way clumsily between the snack bar and lounge chairs. It was after five, and the pool was practically deserted. Down the ladder at the four-foot marker she crept, rung by rung, clad in a onepiece bathing suit, and submerged herself to the neck. As she paddled awkwardly away, I cut around her in tight circles, showing off my skills. In the gritty, golden light her face looked soft and young.

Time oozed like syrup off the tip of a spoon, and as we moved through the water I grew bolder and dove under her and passed behind her. Mostly we stayed in the shallow end, sporting and giggling, though once she ventured into the deep end, grunting like a dog. In the shadow of the threemeter board, she lingered a few seconds, treading water and staring down at the wavy

26

image of her feet, her face glazed and absorbed—looking uncannily like her brother. Then she turned around and, arching her neck like a goose, paddled back toward the ladder. Underwater I watched her intently. Her thighs and calves pumped rhythmically, propelling her small, trim figure. Though her stroke was rusty, it was obvious she was a natural. I followed her underwater all the way to the ladder, till I thought my lungs would burst. Then she got out, and, without looking back at me or the pool, wobbled through the lounge chairs and disappeared inside the hotel.

3.

The next morning, as the water warmed up, I stretched my limbs and blew bubbles out of my mouth. At noon the sun blazed down, sheeting the sky with a blinding light. The trio of Washingtonian palms was starkly outlined against the glare, the fronds drooping like severed tongues. The sound of a slow drip, like oil from a pan, plinked against my ears. The water thinned out, enabling me to see enormous distances, to points much further than the dimensions of the pool. I could make out every feature on the lamp under the diving board. Cracks, smudges, the rungs on the ladders, bits of chipped tile, faded numbers indicating depth stood out in bold relief as though I were surveying them through a telescope. Under my elbow the drain shimmered like a hubcap. The pool wasn't big—twenty yards in length, six or seven yards wide—but the magnifying power of the water made it seem as if the distances were enormous. Sloping up from the drain, the floor of the pool resembled a continental shelf sweeping leisurely toward the rim of a gigantic land mass. Slowly, I inched along it, a water creature from sunken Atlantis—huge and oily and glistening—looking to have a little fun along the shore, surprise a pair of copulating whales or goose a water skier with the tip of my tongue.

Late that afternoon, a group of weekenders from Los Angeles, three families, arrived at the complex. Within minutes their kids were in the pool, splashing water and throwing balls. It didn't take them long to discover me. "Momma!" screamed one kid. "There's a big thing at the bottom of the pool!"

Mrs. Baines trotted over from the manager's office and calmed everybody down. Evidently, my father had told her about my hospital appointment on Monday, because she was willing to let me stay where I was for a few more days. She told the parents that I was a graduate student from UC-Irvine conducting tests on the effect of chlorine on the eyes, and that I wouldn't harm anyone. The parents told the kids, but that didn't prevent them from diving down to gawk at me. At first they shot me the finger and shouted frothy obscenities; then a little girl stroked my thigh, and they all started stroking my thighs and arms. At one point there were five kids around me like pilot fish around a whale, stroking my thighs and chest. Then it was dinner time, and they all had to leave.

That night, it must have been late, Leo crept to the edge of the pool and drew up a chair. There was a hard, ranting edge to his voice. "Sure, you can lie there and not do anything, what's it matter to you? You're well-fixed, you got a father who's left you well off, you can afford to lie at the bottom of a pool...."

Overhead, there was a moon, more than half full. A

28

light wind whipped through the palms, shaking their crowns. An unusual number of birds were out, taking advantage of the illuminated air to chase insects.

" ... I'm not bitter, don't get me wrong ... I don't give a damn what you do. Besides, you're a nice guy, you're well-mannered, you've paid me lots of attention, which not too many people have done in the past, unless they were paid to do it. I don't know what I'm griping about, life's been good to me, I've made dough, not exactly a fortune, but enough to keep me comfortable. I ought to be resting easy, you know? I ought to be sleeping ten hours a night like a kid, but I can't and I'm not. There's something keeps picking at me and won't let up.

"My daughter turned out all right. After a rough start, she settled down, got a decent husband, nothing like the *shtunk* she first married. God knows, I had a few sleepless nights when she was younger. She was a hot one, all right, ready to jump in the sack with a nineiron. I don't know where she got that from ... I wasn't a sex fiend ... God knows, her mother wasn't. Must've been a stray gene she picked up somewhere. My father came from Odessa ... his family was all pretty sensible. Anyway, she's straightened out. She's having a good life now; last year she blessed me with a beautiful granddaughter. So why is it, Navvy, I get up in the middle of the night and come out and talk to you? A guy lying at the bottom of a swimming pool!

"You always was a good listener, Navvy, that's why you and me became friends. You paid attention to me, and old people like that, they like to feel that what they say is important. Nobody has listened to me for seven years, ever since I got out of the business. When I ran the business they had to listen to me, their jobs depended on

29

it, and don't think I didn't talk a blue streak! It was wonderful, Navvy. Unless they had something to say about the business, I didn't pay much attention. Why bother? If it didn't help business, what good was it? Oh, I was a hardass, Navvy, a real hardass.

"But you always listened to me, like I had something to say, like you needed to hear what I said. You reminded me of my cousin Alvah, the guy who became a rabbi. He was a good listener too, one of those inner listeners, a guy who paid lots of attention to what was going on inside himself. Sort of mystical, you might say. Had he lived in Poland in the last century, God forbid, he'd have been a great man, a Talmudic scholar, a visionary. But Chicago in the 1920s was a different place. Onward and upward, onward and upward. For a kid as talented as Alvah to become a rabbi and remain in the ghetto was craziness. But Alvah was crazy, no doubt about it. He read and studied and studied and read. He liked to carry on long conversations with himself. He was forever debating about God, the universe, human nature, instinct versus reason... all that dizzy stuff. He never made a dime in his life. He only had one suit when he died, he rode the bus or subway everywhere, he lived in a shitty two-room apartment in the nigger section, he had no sex life... but he died like a champ, with a look on his face like he'd just seen an angel and shook hands personally. I never seen a person's face look like that when they died, and I've seen a few people die. Calm... sweet. You know what his last words were? 'Keep my gloves on, Leo, I'm sailing out tonight.' I damn near cracked in half. Is that what comes from listening to yourself all those years, Navvy, or was my cousin just an exceptional man? Do all mystics die that way? Or do some die remorseful, begging for another chance?

"Why the hell don't you answer me? You listened politely when I fed you bourbon at my house! Now you've vanished into the water! Was I that boring, Navvy? Was I? Good God, I got to talk to somebody! I got to hear some noise back in return. Thank God this is California and the television goes all night! At least I can hear something! At least I can talk back! I'm going crazy, Navvy. It's been a bad week since you went into the water. I'm upset, your dad's upset, his girlfriend's upset. Say something, Navvy, will you? Kick your leg or let go a bubble, something to let me know you're listening!"

4.

Late at night, after the lamp under the board goes off and I am plunged into watery darkness, I hear voices. I call them voices, though they are not exactly that; they are more like calls or signals, some transmitted over a great distance, other sounding close by, I listen intently. My ears—modest nubs scooping off the sides of my head—strain to catch each utterance. In every one there is a singularity of consciousness that leaves me breathless. Where they come from, I'm not sure. Overhead, in the wavering light of the half-moon, I see bats and night-hawks wheeling after insects. Attracted by the pool's shimmering reflection, the insects zoom into the water. Their cries—a sound like rusty knives being scraped together—dins against my ears. Their carcasses litter the surface. An urgent code, which I have not yet deciphered, runs through their screeches. Survival is what they are mainly concerned with—that much is obvious.

31

Aware of their mutual plight, they call frantically among themselves. Other insects, from the safety of the grass, shout encouragement.

The earwigs—long, black beetles with ferocious pincers—are particularly outspoken. They wail pathetically as soon as they strike the water. Ten or fifteen combine to create a dreary threnody. "Hang on!" I shout. "I'll be right there!" But they don't seem to understand; the sound of my voice only makes them wail louder. Even after I carry them to safety, they continue to protest till the dry night air evaporates the water on their legs, and they scurry off toward the grass.

Amid these lamentations other signals can be heard: the sonic whistling of a bat; nighthawks screeling; the chig-chig-chig of a hungry sparrow hawk; doves warbling elegiacally; the spiny click of a lizard's foot; the stricken call of a quail. Tonight, in homage to the swelling moon, a mockingbird cheers the air from an olive tree. It is such a virtuoso performance that I pause in my search for stranded bugs to listen. An astonishing variety of sounds pours out of its throat—bleeps, chirps, warbles, screeches, whistles, hums, whirrs. Up and down the scale it soars, mixing high and low, flat and sharp, harsh and soft, a dazzling blend of dulcet and fortissimo that leaves me gasping. On the drain an hour later, I can still hear the bird, bruiting the moon's face with undiminished ardor.

The Coachella Valley from Indio to Palm Springs is the bed of an ancient sea that once stretched up from the Gulf of California through the Imperial Valley to the San Gorgonio Pass. The shoreline of this ancient sea, remnants of which were still visible 200 years ago when the Spaniards first passed this way, can be seen on the surrounding mountains. The floor of this evaporated body of water is littered with fossils and the bones of antediluvian creatures. Squatting beside the drain, swallowing water at rhythmic intervals and sluicing it through the slits in my throat, I can hear the remains of these petrified creatures stirring restlessly in the sand. Immersed in a cloudy, particulate solution, I am privy to secrets incommunicable on dry land. Water, the source of all life—even this tiny, chlorinated spot—wakens in me memories of a lush, aquatic past. A pterodactyl croaks overhead. The sound of dinosaurs grazing on the shore creeps distantly to my ears.

It is much later now . . . the moon has disappeared . . . the birds and insects have quieted down. The fronds on the stately Washingtonian palms by the side of the pool function as radar antennae; a host of nebular emissions are snared in their tattered folds. Down the slender, fifty-foot trunks they speed, to the roots, through myriad spongy capillaries, and into the water. Broken up into a series of long and short pulses, the emissions crackle against my ears like an aquatic Morse code. With every impulse my consciousness expands . . . from a fixed point deep in the narrow, kivalike confines of the pool, I am projected out along vectors of countless points radiating across the heavens. Outside becomes in . . . outer, inner . . . space as intimate as water . . . water as infinite as space . . . awareness the unifying yoke . . . concentrated yet diffused . . . dilating in quantum bounds . . . sealed in the heart of a fish!

33

CHAPTER III

1.

Saturday morning Dennis called. He wanted me to come to Dr. Bilkstrode's office that afternoon so he could get some tissue samples before I went into the hospital on Monday. My father gave me the message; he put on one of my suits and walked down to the pool and jumped into the water. Imagine my surprise when I saw him hovering over me, grinning and giving the thumbs-up sign. He hadn't been swimming in twenty years.

At Bilkstrode's office I was ushered into an examination room and told to take off my clothes and put on a smock. Photos of dead armadillos adorned the yellow walls—squashed by trucks, punctured by stakes, perforated by bullets, poisoned by herbicides. There must have been twenty of them, glossy and highlighted by gruesome details, each carefully composed with the professional skill of a police photographer.

"Thanks very much for coming in on such short notice," Dennis said, breezing through the sliding door and giving my hand a shake. "We need to determine the texture and chemical make-up of your skin. We can do that here as easily as they can over at Eisenhower Medical, plus we'll save time."

His mustache bothered me. His mouth was small and tight, and the mustache drooped over his upper lip like thatching on a Tudor cottage. His hair was long and combed in layers that swept over his ears. He gazed at me earnestly but without any real interest beyond the symptoms of my so-called affliction.

"You're very important to us because with each new patient we learn more about the disease. The Evtuffel Syndrome has become a specialty of ours. We believe it to be the disease of the future. Someday it's going to be more commonplace than cancer."

"You've made the wrong diagnosis on me."

"What do you mean?"

"I'm not a victim of the Evtuffel Syndrome."

"Well, I hate to disillusion you, but—"

"I've done this to myself," I said firmly.

"Pardon?"

"I've given myself this green skin... these gills."

"Well, of course, that's what you want to think."

"I wanted this... it's my creation. Metamorphosing into a fish was an act of will. I have willed it myself."

"You are a very naive boy."

Coming from a man my own age, this was intolerable. "If I want to make myself into a blackbird, I will make myself into a blackbird," I snarled, trying to control my voice. "If I want to make myself into an otter, I'll make myself into an otter."

"That's hokum. You can't be serious."

A sudden rush of anxiety hobbled my tongue. "I... I don't mean I... can do it all... alone," I stammered. "I need help... guidance."

"Dr. Frantz Evtuffel was a sensitive and perceptive man. His discoveries about the reactive mechanisms of the human mind and their effect on the body rival those of Freud."

36

"Piss on Freud!" I shouted. "I'm responsible for the form I take! The shit in the air has nothing to do with it! You can't stand the fact that I might be autonomous! You want me to be a victim, like all the other victims, so you can label the symptoms to fit your diagnosis! You and that fat ghoul, Bilkstrode!"

Dennis stood stock-still, quivering like a reed; then he turned on his heel and marched from the room. A moment later a pair of burly assistants entered with a cart, strapped me to it, and whisked me down a corridor reeking of lime and disinfectant. In an operating room they transferred me to a table and bound me tightly at the chest, hips, and ankles with leather belts.

A squad of smocked attendants hovered over me, plucking tissue samples from my skin with sharp little instruments resembling lemon peelers. They didn't bother with an anesthetic; they merely rubbed the desired spot with alcohol and gouged out morsels of flesh an inch long and a quarter of an inch thick which they deposited into a stainless steel bowl. After collecting a dozen samples, they applied a salve to each wound and told me to lie still for twenty minutes. Then they gathered up their tools and filed out of the room, snapping off the light.

I lay in the dark, blinking back hot tears. The holes in my chest and legs burned miserably.

"Be brave..."

"Huh?"

"It will hurt for awhile, then it will go away."

The voice, coarsened by too many cigarettes, sounded familiar. "Who... are you?" I called.

"Even old script girls have their secrets..."

"Hetty?... Hetty!... Is that you?"

37

"On the table beside you. They did to me earlier what they just did to you. I got the mange again, only they call it the Evfluffle Syndrome, or some damn stupid thing."

Despite the fiery wounds in my body, I rolled over to my left, straining against the belts, and peered into the darkness. A ghostly figure, shrouded in a sheet, lay on another table ten feet away. Gradually, my eyes adjusted, and I could see her face, Hetty's face, peering over at me.

"I didn't see you when I came in."

"They don't give you much of a chance to see anything," she said.

"But... I didn't know you had..."

"Oh sure. Had it for years. Not what they think, of course."

"But at the party...?"

"I looked fine. I still look fine. A little green around the jaw maybe. My children don't like it when I turn green. Whenever I do, they drag me from the pool and carry me into Bilkstrode's office."

"You have a pool!"

"Of course, dearie. This is Southern California, isn't it?"

"But... I mean... you spend lots of time in your pool...?"

"Lots. When I get these spells I refuse to come out. This time, while I'm in the hospital, my daughter has threatened to fill up the pool with cement."

She sighed. "Some women my age get face lifts. I get my skin bleached."

"What's it like?"

"Awful. They put you in a big tank filled with sponges and squeeze you till you faint. Then they plunge you in a sauna and cook you till all the juices are gone. By that time they can do anything they want with you."

"Hetty, I won't let them do this to me."

"I know. When I saw you at the party I knew you were in a pickle. Your father doesn't like machinery that doesn't run properly. When something's broken, it's got to get fixed. Before Andrea came along, he and I had a little romance."

"I didn't know that . . ."

"You were in Kansas City. But I guess I lost interest, or maybe he did. Anyway, he got annoyed when I wouldn't get out of the pool to mix him a drink one day. When I finally did, he took one look and called an ambulance."

"Then you've seen Bilkstrode before?"

"Oh, God, yes! And each time he thinks he's cured me. He thinks I'm tense about something . . . anxious. I'm long past menopause, so it can't be that. He just doesn't realize how much I like the water. Water is the only cure for this affliction, and lots of it. That's why, when I saw you at the party, I dragged you off to the tub."

"And it worked," I sighed. "My skin got so dry and itchy with all those people."

"Bilkstrode can get rid of that. But, if you're like me, it will come back."

I flailed helplessly against the straps. "Of course it will come back! Because it's not what those jerks think it is! You haven't got the mange, Hetty, and you're not tense! You're turning into something totally beyond their comprehension."

"I've often wondered what was happening to me. I never really worried about it because it always felt so good. When I'm in the water I have no worries about

39

anything; I become so interested in everything around me. I love to just lie there and listen. I can do that for hours. It's amazing what you can hear. It's amazing what comes to you when you let yourself relax like that."

"Yes . . . yes," I said breathlessly. "What I hope eventually is to evolve a telepathic process whereby I can talk back to the creatures who are talking to me. I want them to know that I am receiving their signals and want to hear more. Maybe if they're aware that I'm listening, they'll communicate more freely. I must get word to them. I must!"

Voices sounded in the hallway, harsh and threatening.

"Be brave," she whispered. "The water has taught me a trick or two. Maybe I can do something."

2.

"Still lying there, Navvy?" asked a familiar voice.

I moaned and thrashed my legs. It was Leo, middle of the night, punctual as a freight train.

"It isn't easy for me to come out every night and see you lying on the drain. It makes me think you're lazy. I had an employee once, Buster Silvestre was his name. Every break he'd get up from his machine and stretch out on a box at the back of the room. Lunch hour he'd stretch out on the box and eat lying down. 'Buster,' I'd say, 'How come you lie down all the time during your breaks? It's bad for your digestion to eat lying down.' 'Mr. Kropotnik,' he'd say, 'this is the only time of the day when you don't own me. When I lie down this way, I can think better.' 'And just what have you got to think about, Buster?' I'd say. 'Myself,' he'd say. 'This is the only time

40

during the day when I can think about myself and not about your goddamn pants . . . '

"Is that why you lie down there, Navvy, so you can think better about yourself? Can you reach yourself easier in the water? What is it about the water that makes it easier to reach yourself? I swim every day, and no thoughts occur to me in the pool that I don't have out of it. I think of business in the pool same as I do out of it, same as I do anywhere. I'm a businessman . . . am I supposed to have other thoughts in the water? Am I supposed to think of women instead?

"People used to listen to me. They had to; I was their boss. 'Yes, Mr. Kropotnik,' they'd say. 'No, Mr. Kropotnik.' I commanded respect; I owned the company. They listened eagerly to what I had to say. 'Yes, sir . . . no, sir.'

"Nobody listens to me now. I can't pay anybody to listen to me now. My wife, she used to listen to me, but she's dead now, and she can't listen anymore. I like to be listened to, Navvy, even when I'm not sure what I want to say. If you was to come up out of the water right now and say, 'Okay, Leo, I want to listen to you,' I don't think I'd know what to say. Maybe I'd start off by telling you about my father, what a remarkable man he was, about how he left Odessa when he was fifteen years old and came to the United States to find a better life. I'd tell you about him. And my mother. She was a great lady. She had her bad times, but she was awful good to my brothers and me. If you was here right now, sitting on the steps with your head out of the water, I'd tell you plenty. I got lots of names and dates in my head. I never forget a name or a date. I can tell you the date of my *bar mitzvah* . . . November 12, 1917. I can tell you the day I first opened my pants shop . . . July 14, 1931. Middle of

41

the Depression, Navvy, and don't think that wasn't tough! I can tell you the day my daughter took her first steps... April 2, 1946. Oh, I got the dates, all the facts, right at my fingertips. I'm plenty smart that way.

"I like people who nod and don't say anything. Those are the kind of listeners I like. I don't want them to question what I say; I just want them to listen. The best listener is the one who nods and says okay and lets you go your way. It's tough to be a good listener. My cousin Alvah used to say that you had to enjoy listening to yourself before you could listen to anybody else. Since I retired, I've tried that. Late at night I turn off the TV and come out here by the pool and lie down on a chair like Buster Silvestre used to do in the back of my shop during lunch hour. But all I hear is static. Like static on the radio, that's all I get, crackle crackle crackle. I listen as hard as I can, and that's all I hear.

"Is that what you hear down there, Navvy? Static? Wish to God I could get this crackling out of my head. The only thing that helps is the crackling from the television which neutralizes the crackling in my ears. Only with the goddamn TV blaring can I get some sleep. The two cracklings cancel each other out. Crackle-crackle, crackle-crackle.

"If you don't come up out of the water, Navvy, I'm gonna dive down there and pull you up by the hair. You're being rude. What gives you the right to act so independent? What makes you think you can escape the crackling? Not as long as you live will you ever escape it. You'll still hear it at the bottom of the pool, because I'm here to remind you of it. You can't take a breath without hearing static. You say you want to flush yourself out so you won't hear any more static, and I say that's ridicu-

42

lous. You were born hearing static and you're going to hear it the rest of your life.

"You know, when I was a young man first in business I used to get very nervous about whether I would make it or not. I had lots of reasons to be worried—it was the middle of the Depression, Now, forty-five years later, I remember that nervousness with great affection. It was my own. I carried it around with me all day; I took it to bed with me at night. But it was my own, that was the difference. I chose it for myself—like my wife, my daughter, my house, my car, all the things I ever loved and wanted, it was mine and I was responsible for it.

"But things are different today. People have to bear an extra weight. In addition to their own nervousness, they have to bear each other's nervousness. Television has brought other people's problems into our lives. In addition to coping with our own nervousness, we have to cope with theirs. And that's unfair. Life is hard enough without having to suffer what other people are nervous about. No wonder nobody wants to listen to anybody else. No wonder they want to disappear under the water and never come up."

3.

Sunday evening I crawled out of the water and went up to the house to get something to eat. On the kitchen table I found a note. "Andrea and I are at Melvyn's for dinner. I will come get you in the morning."

I didn't want to think about it, so I dried off and fixed a big bowl of cottage cheese and spinach salad and sprinkled in some garbanzo beans and sunflower seeds. I

43

had the bowl up to my face and was nibbling on the leaves when the phone rang. My webbed fingers closed clumsily around the receiver.

"Navvy, I'm glad I reached you . . ."

"Hetty?"

"Yes. Can you meet me at Ruth Hardy Park in Palm Springs . . . ?"

"Sure."

"In one hour?"

"Okay."

"I've got something that might help you."

"Great. I was thinking of running away to the Salton Sea."

"No-oo! Your skin isn't tough enough. That's an incorrigible body of water . . ."

"I don't want to go to the hospital tomorrow, Hetty."

"And you won't have to if you get into town and meet me in the park in an hour."

"Really?"

"Be quick about it!"

"I'm on my way."

I finished eating and looked around for something to wear. In the hall closet, I found a polyester leisure suit, with long sleeves and a zipper up the front. Andrea had given it to my father for his birthday, and he never wore it. I concealed my gills by turning up the collar and covered my glossy hair with a golf cap. The wet smell I muffled as best I could with a handful of aftershave lotion.

I hitchhiked into Palm Springs. Fortunately, it was almost dark, so the guy and girl who picked me up in their van didn't notice my green skin. I made small talk, punctuating every third or fourth word with a resonant click that welled up from my chest. This amused them, and they started clicking and grunting in unison. Spasms of laughter followed each effort, and finally the guy had to pull the car over and dry his eyes and wipe his nose. The girl fell onto the mattress in the back of the van and began hiccupping violently. I was glad to get out downtown and escape into the night.

From Palm Canyon Drive I walked over to Ruth Hardy Park. A marine band from Twenty-Nine Palms was playing in the gazebo. A hot dragon wind rattled through the trees. Despite the heat, the park was crowded, old folks sitting in folding chairs and fanning themselves with programs, youngsters sprawled on blankets. The marines, togged out in khaki shirts and shiny blue trousers, were galloping through a John Philip Sousa march. I located the Big Dipper in the west, tipped on its lip as though emptying directly onto the Los Angeles basin. In the heat the stars seemed dull and lifeless, like bits of gravel. I steered around the crowd to the back and finally settled under the spiny branches of a paloverde tree.

The number coming up was entitled "Revolt: 1680," a suite in three parts by marine composer Franklin A. Garvis. A note on the program said that Garvis was born in New Mexico of Pueblo Indian parents in 1932 and died on the outskirts of Hue in the winter of 1968, the victim of a sniper bullet. Despite a lifelong career in the marines, Garvis never rose higher in rank than sergeant. Conservatory-trained in Albuquerque and Los Angeles, he devoted his off-duty time to composing original scores for military bands. The most talented composer to come out of the marines, perhaps all the Armed Forces, he wrote in a powerful, accented style embodying many of the rhythms of his Pueblo Indian heritage.

The piece opened with a whisper of wire brushes across a snare, accompanied by a castanet-like clicking. Squealing saxophone riffs were swallowed up in a snarl of brass as the tempo quickly accelerated. Glissading fanfares by the trombone section announced the moment when the Pueblos revolted against their Spanish overlords. Thundering tom-toms, splashed with cymbals, joined a chorus of gnashing trumpets as the revolt fanned from village to village, and the Pueblos began massacring every white person in the Rio Grande Valley.

The music pulsed through my veins, rousing my blood to a feverish pitch. A furious scream clamored in my throat, which I stifled with my hand. Fists clenched, I rolled to my knees. But before I could move, a gentle but implacable pressure forced me down. Turning, I saw Hetty, or what looked like Hetty, a woman with Hetty's face dressed in a white terrycloth robe, standing over me. In the dim light, her eyes burned like rivets.

"Save your energy," she whispered in a voice that stung my ears. "That kind of violence has nothing to do with you. It happened a long time ago and belongs to a period of history you had no part in. Make sure when you do battle that that battle is your own. The demons of history enjoy fighting their battles over and over in the bodies of young men who do not know what has possessed them, or why. If you change your form as you say you want to, you will deny them access to your mind and body forever, and whatever violence you find in life will be of your own making and for your own reasons."

"Hetty? . . . Hetty? . . . Is that you?"

The face moved closer. It was Hetty's jaw, all right, the loose flesh sagging in an arc; but the eyes belonged to

46

another creature, a dragonfly perhaps—round, bulging eyes.

Scooping her hands under my arms, she lifted me to my feet. The voice was Hetty's, raspy from too many cigarettes, but invigorated with a hissing urgency. "After I left Bilkstrode's office, I went home and got into the pool. My daughter tried to stop me, but I chased her away with a golf club. In the water, I thought and thought about how you might be able to defend yourself against your father. All night I thought about this question, searching for an answer. Finally, it came to me, from where I'm not sure, but through the water very clear."

"Yes . . . yes?"

"There is a message waiting for you a long way off. If you find it, you will learn how to communicate with all creatures, living and dead. And once you have that, your power will be so great that you will never have to fear your father or Dr. Bilkstrode again."

"Where is the message?"

"In Mexico. In Ensenada."

"Ensenada! That's a long way off! I'll never get there looking like I do now. My feet are too clumsy. The heat will kill me."

"I can help you acquire the human form you had before you entered the water," she said. "But only for a short time. One week at the most. You must go over the mountains to the coast and then down to Ensenada. The message is there."

"Where in Ensenada will I find it?"

"By the sea, off the Avenida Primera, there is a park, a place of great honor for the Mexican people. In it is a large bust, twelve feet high, forged out of iron and plated with

47

gold. It is the face of one of Mexico's great heroes—Miguel Hidalgo. Hidden in the folds of the golden beard is a message."

"Ah!"

"Take this..." She held out a small silver object, rounded, like a needle, in a half moon. "...clamp it under your tongue, against the tendon that ties your tongue to your mouth. Keep it there all night. Keep it there for the rest of the week, until midnight next Sunday."

"Where did you get it?"

"I've had it for years, but I never knew what it was for until I listened in the water. It's called a tongue-stick, and it once belonged to my great-grandmother. She was a Shaker from Indiana, and they used it on children who, for one reason or another, had difficulty speaking. The pressure on the base of the tongue assuaged the children's fears and enabled them to speak in their own voices... unique to themselves but recognizable to everyone."

"How do you know it will work on me?"

She put her hands on my shoulders and swept my face with her churning eyes. She radiated so much power that I became frightened and shied backward from her grasp, but she gripped me firmly and pushed me into the paloverde tree till my back bumped against the smooth trunk, and I had to stare her full in the face. "The secrets revealed in the water are unlike any others. They come from sources too deep to be reached by ordinary understanding... all I can do is open the portals leading in their direction and wait for them to rise to me. I have immersed myself, and I have heard. *That* is how I know."

I gulped and tried to stammer out my gratitude, but

48

she pinched my mouth shut. "Go home and sleep. When you wake up, you'll look like you did before you entered the water. But only for a week. You start for Ensañada tomorrow."

4.

Voices again... familiar, comforting. Bats screeling, nighthawks jabbering, mockingbirds caroling. Within twenty feet of the pool, overhead and to either side, a wealth of secret, invisible life. The sound of moonlight hissing faintly on the pool's surface. Rattle of palm fronds from the stately Washingtonians. Earwigs drilling narrow tunnels through the sand. Comfortable, familiar sounds pattering against my ears. The drain is an umbilicus connecting me with all creatures, all objects. Plugged into it, if only tenuously by the rubbery weight of my hip, I am privy to rare and fabulous communiqués.

Further afield, out on the desert floor, other sounds—hushed, alien, insistent—settle through the primary layer of domestic utterances like raindrops through a screen of leaves. Moonlight washes the sandy wastes with an eerie, milky solution, highlighting clumps of sage, stands of ocotillo, sprigs of creosote and jimson. Shadows ink the rifts between their brittle frames, lending an illusion of solidity till they resemble coral formations. Mice and kangaroo rats creep around the roots, nibbling seeds. Sidewinders coil in tight hieroglyphs; lizards knock blindly against one another; a screech owl pierces a furry object with its talons; jackrabbits copulate with vigorous strokes.

Further afield, out in the dry, sandy hills beyond

49

Indio, come mutterings and ruminations from fossils and ichthyosaurs, bones of aboriginal Indians, the petrified beaks of entombed pterodactyls, remnants of blood and movement and spirit that once populated the valley. They call to me familiarly, ally and old friend, a fellow submergent, purveyor of underwater secrets, and I stir restlessly, longing to answer back in a familiar tongue, to reassure them that someday the fabled waters of the Sea of Cortez will come gushing up the Imperial Valley and rouse them from their long, dry sleep. Perhaps, in the shuddering wake of an earthquake, the seam, formed by centuries of Rocky Mountain silt brought down by the rampaging Colorado, will rip right open from Yuma to Palm Springs, a wide, yawning funnel through which the spumy current will rush to soften their petrified shells and frigid tentacles and give them life again.

Further afield I hear the bubbling of a drowned Japanese submarine and its crew, sunk off the tip of Baja California. The voices plaintive and dignified, redolent with fidelity to emperor and homeland. Each man still at his station, tense and alert, as when the depth charge struck the conning tower. The influx of water was so swift and devastating there was no time to react, and each man died transfixed, with a hand clutching a gauge or lever, staring down between his legs. Over this, surging with convulsive force, comes the groan of mating whales in Scanlon's Bay, a frothy, ecstatic paean that sends shivers rippling across my vulcanized hide. And further afield, warbly and quavering, the voices of legendary poets, drowned through mishap or design: Hart Crane crying through the Gulf Stream off Key West; Percy Shelley warding off ravenous fish in the Ligurian Sea; Virginia Woolf, pockets loaded with stones, mad

with the voices of fellow victims, marching fully clothed into the reedy depths of the River Ouse. And even further afield, faint but unmistakable, the thrumming of intergalactic constellations radiating raw energy, the sound of suns being born and dying, the bombastic reverberation of planetary expansion, a massive nebular upheaval rachetting across millions of miles of space to plink against the palm frond receptors and trickle into the water, a charged electric whisper, diminished but inexhaustible. And furthest afield, at the ultimate reaches of the universe, a most terrifying sound, a nonsound, the echoless din of dead space, the drone of a black hole, no bigger than a gumdrop, a spot of concentrated malevolence continually devouring itself, the residue of a collapsed star, which moves through the universe like a murderous shark, gobbling everything in its path . . . .
. . . .
. . . .
. . . .
. . . .
. . . .
. . . .

A vigorous pounding jolted me out of my reverie. Leo, wearing a diving mask, his eyes streaked and bugging behind the plate of tempered glass, attacked me with both fists, his thin mouth pouring out a spate of angry bubbles. When he ran out of breath, I collared him around the neck and dragged him to the steps. In the bedroom of his tiny bungalow I finally calmed him down and listened sympathetically to his griefstricken babbling till the moon went down and the mockingbirds stopped cheering the soft night air.

CHAPTER IV

1.

Monday morning, wet and dripping, I crawled from the water to find that I had changed back into an ordinary human. My skin was soft and smooth, the webbing had disappeared between my toes, my chest had shrunk to normal.

Dawn was just breaking over the valley, a brilliant profusion of orange and pink rays, as I walked up to the house. I tiptoed into my bedroom and threw some clothes into a duffel bag. After consuming a bowl of granola, a banana, and two pieces of toast, I wrote a note to my father and slipped it under the door of his bedroom: "Dad, gone to Enseñada to check on a beard. Be back in a few days."

An old hermit in a donkey cart was plodding up Highway 74 into the mountains. I hailed him, and he offered me a ride. "Whar you headed fer, sonny?" he barked.

"Enseñada."

"Ben thar mesef oncet, back in 1937. Purty harbor. Mexes treat you right well. Wonder if the road tween thar an Tijuanny's been fixed yet?"

"I wouldn't know."

"Business or pleasure?"

"A little of both."

53

"That's the way to keep it."

He slapped the reins against the donkey and we started up the mountain. The donkey was old and gray, with fly-encrusted haunches and ears like an antelope. Cloudy specks streaked its baleful eyes; a mouthful of spintered teeth poked up off a wedge of rotten gum. But the beast was indefatigable; up and up it plodded, heaving determinedly against the traces. Every few yards the hermit leaped out and fed the animal an apple or a cupcake.

Halfway up the mountain, we both hopped out and hoofed alongside the cart. Cars whizzed by, air-conditioned Lincolns and Cadillacs, heading for the coast, leaving a spoor of engine coolant on the smoldering road. It was only eight o'clock, but the sun was hot as a frying pan, and the heat rolling off the asphalt parched my tender cheeks. But I felt strong and confident, on my way, at last, to Enseñada. When the old hermit broke into a song, I hummed along and clapped my hands:

> I ain't in no hurry
> I ain't in no rush
> My name's Awful Andy
> And I'm King of the Brush.

"Hey, Awful, how long you lived up on these rocks?"

"Since '45, sonny, the autumn of '45, when the Chi Cubs lost the series to them Tiggers."

It was a forbidding place, outcropping after outcropping of bare chocolate rock, with stalks of yucca pronging up from the cracks and fissures.

"What do you do up here?"

"Work my whistle, sonny, work my whistle."

54

Presently the road leveled off, we hopped back into the cart, and I found out what he meant. Looping the reins around his wrist, he pinched his tongue between his hard, horny fingers and pulled it a good six inches out of his mouth. Taking a deep breath, he blew down hard and began valving the fat, pink muscle. A high, nasal sound like the whine of a bagpipe curled around my ears. The donkey raised its head and brayed loudly, to which Awful responded with a rollicking trill that clamored off the stark brown rocks. Between toots, he flexed his fingers, and I saw that the top of his tongue was scored with a half-dozen tiny holes.

"That's some instrument," I marveled.

"Fixed it mesef," said Awful. "Most folks tongues'er thick, but mine's holler, with a tube leadin recollectly to muh windpipe. These lonely nites unner a full moon I purtenear whistle the sadness plum outta these ole bones."

At an overlook we paused to enjoy a stunning view of the valley. Away from our feet the highway switched back and forth a dozen times until it reached the sandy floor and unraveled in a straight line toward Palm Desert. Orchards of date palms swept in rippling waves out toward the railroad tracks. On both sides of Highway 111 were oases of patios and houses. I located the complex where my father lived and the pool, an aquamarine spot shimmering in the morning sun. My throat went dry and a feeling of sadness overwhelmed me, so I crawled back into the cart.

An hour later, in a valley behind the first ridge of the Santa Rosas, Awful Andy guided the cart off the highway toward a stone hovel nestled under a ledge. "This it it fer me, sonny. I got my groceries, my Dodger schedule,

55

an I'm fixin to settle in a spell."

"Appreciate the lift, old timer."

"You go on about ten miles further to Paradise Valley, you'll find an airstrip there. Ever so often, mebbe twice a week, there's some old crate leavin fer the coast. It's a downhill ride, sonny, all the way to the surf, so keep yer britches buttoned."

"Thanks very much."

The donkey brayed apoplectically. "Good luck, sonny, an when you find yer new voice come back an play a tune with me."

"I will. Good-bye."

Walking with my thumb out, it wasn't long until I got a lift in an oil truck. The driver was a muscular fellow in his late thirties, wearing Levis and a tank top. His arms, shoulders, and chest were tattooed with the logos of the major oil companies. Round blue initials, spelling O-P-E-C, formed a livid necklace across the base of his throat. "I know where my money is, hunky, you can bet on that!" he roared over the throbbing diesel. "No way in the world the big grease is gonna let sun or atom power break up their monopoly! Them and the Rabs got the world by the scrots, and they got mighty long fingernails to boot!"

"That's very interesting," I said.

"Where you off to?"

"Enseñada."

"Ha Ha Ha! When we run outta oil, all we gotta do is round up a few Mexes, squeeze em in a vise, and we got enough grease to lube every motor west of the Rockies."

"I think I'll be going," I said, opening the door.

"Take it easy, little man, I was just kiddin. Them Mexes is okay, they got their own way of walkin. Where

56

you from anyway?"

"I live in a swimming pool in the desert."

"Good a place as any in this day and age."

Just before the Paradise Valley turnoff we passed through a terrible brush fire that raged up and down the mountains on both sides of the highway. Thousands of fire fighters from all over Southern California were trying to beat back the blaze with wet towels and blankets. At a roadblock we were warned that we could negotiate the next three miles at our own peril.

"I got oil to git through, podna, to Idyllwild!"

The cops eyes were pearly and red-rimmed with smoke. "Good luck," he sighed.

The truck shot through the roadblock, knocking aside barriers like ninepins. Around a curve we roared, gathering speed, scattering small game huddled on the concrete for safety. The fire encroached on the shoulder, nibbling at the asphalt. Manzanita sprigs, glowing like party streamers, pelted the heavy rig. I gulped and dug my fingers into the seat. Chomping a cigarette, Big Grease shifted into sixth and stomped the accelerator. With a thunderous roar, the truck shot straight into the inferno. Around another bend a canopy of fire hovered over the road, low enough to singe a gopher's fur. I stuffed my fingers down my throat to choke off a scream. Straddling the yellow line, Big Grease blew through the layer, with fire scurfing across the cab roof and lapping at the wheels. A long minute later we emerged on the other side to the wide-eyed stares of another army of aesbestos-clad fire fighters armed with rakes and shovels. A gaunt figure with blistered cheeks shouted angrily through a megaphone, while his fellow workers cheered and waved their implements like peasants at the close of a successful uprising.

At the turnoff, Big Grease slowed the truck. "Couple of miles over that hill and into the valley, you'll find Paradise Valley," he said. "Pretty place, but I don't call there much anymore. Too many goddamn windmills."

"Thanks, Big Grease. I don't think much of your politics, but you're one hell of a man."

"Ain't life a bitch!" he roared. "Give them Mexes a squeeze for me!"

I bid him farewell and started up the road. Behind me, the sky was greasy with smoke. Ahead, the air was clear and blue; a cool breeze, laced with salty freshets, swept over my cheeks. I had reached a plateau in the middle of the coast range where the weather was mild. Refreshed, I shifted my duffel to my other shoulder and lengthened my stride. The sun beamed down softly, dappling my face and hands. Fields of golden hay ladled out from the roadside. Redwing blackbirds skipped from stalk to stalk. In the middle of a field, about a half-mile from the road, stood a granite boulder, scarred with petroglyphs. Figures of people lying down, a bird with ferocious talons, an enormous grinning gopher marked the rock in an unmistakable tableau.

The entrance to the Witiki reservation was a mile or so beyond. Awful Andy told me they were a mysterious bunch, surly and suspicious, but friendly underneath. Their reservation was sacred ground, so I proceeded cautiously. The Witikis worshipped rocks, ate birds, and lived to be very old, especially the women.

A gate at the entrance stopped me. A pair of carbine-toting guards frisked me thoroughly. Everything—money, passport, wallet, change—was removed from my pockets and placed in a manila envelope. The contents were noted down on the outside by a haggard old squaw dressed in a feathered gown with a necklace fashioned from the bills of a hundred ruby-throated hummingbirds. "How long are you planning to stay?" she asked coldly.

"Why... uh... not long at all. Just as long as it takes me to get to the other side. I am a traveler from the desert on my way to Enseñada. I mean no harm and will cross your land as quickly as possible."

"We will escort you," she said.

Flanked by the guards, we struck away from the highway along a wide path that wound through another field of hay and up a low hill strewn with rocks and small boulders. As we climbed the path, I kept looking back over my shoulder at the big rock behind me which I had seen from the highway. At this angle, new figures appeared, ones I hadn't seen from the road. "What is that?" I said finally after we reached the top of the hill and halted to catch our breath. "That rock back there."

"Underneath is the entrance to our world," said the woman. "It is outside the reservation proper, but it contains the main shaft leading to our homes." In the gentle sunlight her face was stolid and impassive, a mass of hard, muddy wrinkles.

"You live underground?"

"Do you see any dwellings on top?"

I looked around. Down the hill to the east there was nothing but a bare slope shingled with rocks and boulders leading to a field of golden hay. To the west, the hill slanted down through a growth of chaparral to another gate across the highway a mile distant. "You mean this is all the larger your land is?"

"Yes. But it goes very deep."

59

"I live under the surface too, so to speak. In a swimming pool." And I explained to her, briefly, about my father, the Evtuffel Syndrome, Hetty, and my journey to Enseñada. She listened solemnly, her face betraying little sign of interest.

Afterwards, at her invitation, we adjourned to the first level of subterranean digs, a pit with steep sides gouged out in the center of a stand of smoke trees and shielded by their branches. Inside there were holes that opened into a half-dozen tunnels, down which I was forbidden to go. The pit, a halfway station between above and below, was where all guests and Anglo officials were entertained. The bodies of dead birds lay everywhere. Swart-faced girls with flashing fingers were busy plucking them and depositing the feathers into straw baskets. The branches of the smoke trees latticed the interior with a patchwork of shadows. After we sat down, the face of the old squaw grew soft and warm. Over a glass of hot *popotillo* tea, she told me about the Witikis and their history.

"Long ago, Honeyface (she called me), a great lizard-bird got tired of flying around all day looking for food. He thought it would be better to live on the ground where there was food everywhere, instead of having to fly long distances to find it. So he asked Ninpan, Spirit of the Earth and Sky, if He couldn't turn him into a gopher or a rabbit.

"'Why do you want this thing?' said Ninpan. 'You already are a wonderful creature, big and proud and fearsome, and now you want to become an earthling, and be small and vulnerable and covered with dirt.'

"'It is simple, Great Father,' said the lizard-bird. 'I am tired of seeing with my eyes the same features of the land, the mountains, and the sky. They are unchanging. In cold weather they look the same as in warm weather. Their color may change but their form does not. I want to be able to change the form of things. I want to have a vision that will enable me to alter the outline of anything I see. Up in the sky I can't do that. In the open, in the sunlight, things remain as you first see them. That is the way it has always been, and that is the way it will always be. But down in the ground it is different. My friend Gopher tells me that every time he goes underground he sees the most astonishing things. He travels along a hundred tunnels a day, but every tunnel he enters is different. And every time he enters the same tunnel, no matter how many times he's entered it before, it is different. That is the way I would like to see things.'

"'That is a strange request,' said Ninpan. 'Let me think about it, and I will let you know.'

"So Ninpan sat on that rock out there that you saw from the road and thought and thought about it. Then, after a long time, he called to the lizard-bird. 'I will grant your request,' he said, 'on condition that you do something for me in return.'

"'And what is that, O Mighty One?'

"'In the foothills of those mountains over there live a tribe of unruly grub-eaters who lead loose and immoral lives and who terrorize the other good people of this country. In bad times, they share none of their food; in good times, they are always trying to steal. They are ugly, savage people, without good manners, and full of deceitful, thieving ways. I want you to punish them. I want you to fly over there and pick them up in your beak and carry them high up in the air and drop them. That way we will teach them a lesson. The fall will crack open

61

their bodies and release the evil spirits inside. They cannot do it themselves, so we will have to do it for them. After you have dropped them all, I want you to hover over the broken bodies and flap your wings as hard as you can and scatter the evil spirits so they will never again enter their bodies.'

"So the lizard-bird did as he was bid. He flew over to the foothills and picked up the people in his beak and flew back to this spot and dropped them from a very great height. The impact of their bodies against the earth cracked them open and released the evil spirits inside. After he had dropped them all, the lizard-bird swooped down and fanned the ground with his huge wings and scattered the evil spirits to the ends of the world. Then Ninpan came along and with his healing mouth put the people back together again and told them that from that time on they were to live underground. Then he changed the lizard-bird into a clumsy burrowing animal with heavy claws and shaggy hair and made him the leader of the Witiki tribe. The first thing the people did in their new home was to tell the story of what happened to them on that big rock out there that you saw from the road. And that's how the lizard-bird disappeared from the sky, and that's how the Witiki tribe began."

I finished my tea in thoughtful silence.

"You are very young but very earnest," she said, studying my face. "I can tell that by your eyes and by your mouth. The mouth contains the secrets of your past, the eyes the message of your future. You are in for some hard times, Honeyface, but I suspect you know that."

"Yes. Yes, I do."

"Here," she said, slipping a flat, oval object made out

of a polished abalone shell into my palm.

"What is it?"

"A whistle. In case you need it. It has special powers. Use it only when you can no longer trust the sound of your own voice. It can stop people in their tracks. But use it only once, and only when you think you are in the greatest danger. I hope that never happens."

"Thank you, Mother."

"Ninpan be with you, Honeyface, and when you discover the secret of many tongues come speak them to us. Everything on this Holy Earth we are interested in."

2.

At the airstrip there were a couple of piper cubs, a crop duster, an old Cessna, and a ten-passenger glider of World War II vintage. The nose of the glider swung up on hinges to permit entry. People were already queuing up, mainly ranchers and their wives with a chaotic assortment of ducks, geese, hens, turkeys, and pigeons, on their way to the market in La Jolla. The pilot, decked out in jodhpurs, scarf, and goggles, grinned politely. "Where are you headed, señor?" Across the breast of his leather flight jacket was stencilled the name ANZA.

"Enseñada."

"Can't take you that far. This crate's only going to the coast."

"That's fine."

"Cost you four bucks."

"How do you get this thing off the ground with no motor?" I asked after I paid him.

"There's a cable tied to the nose that's attached to a

winch at the end of the strip. Beyond that is a 400-foot cliff kissed by thermals from the coast. We shoot over that, the wind picks us up, and it's all downhill from there."

He was a handsome man of Latin extraction, with skin smooth as an armpatch, a mustache like a caterpillar, and piercing brown eyes.

Before settling in the pilot's seat, Anza handed out cyanide capsules. "In case there's no wind when the winch catapults us over the cliff," he explained. "You can take it cold, or crunch this between your teeth and you'll be dead before we hit the rocks."

The other passengers calmly held the capsules in their hands; they had made the trip before.

"Hey . . . you . . . Sweetcheeks," Anza said, motioning to me. "You sit up front with me. There's no hydraulic on the rudders, and I need some muscle power."

I climbed into the copilot's seat and took hold of the wheel. Anza belted me in and patted my forehead. "When I say *now,* pull back on the stick and press both feet down on the pedals."

"What'll I do with this?" I said, indicating the cyanide.

"Put it under your tongue. Just don't bite down."

"How long have you been doing this?"

"I've made hundreds of flights. Don't worry, *hombre,* we'll make it. See that wind socket over there? As long as it's full of air, we have no problem."

The wind socket stuck out stiffly at right angles from the pole.

At a signal from Anza, a crewman at the end of the strip engaged the winch. Slowly, we trundled forward, the craft shaking and bumping along the uneven ground on little rubber wheels. The poultry began clucking suspiciously; the other passengers braced their feet and raised the cyanide to their lips. Faster and faster we sped, the ground-speed indicator on the cockpit panel climbing quickly past 40, 50, 60 miles an hour. My asshole cinched tighter than a lariat knot. I gripped the copilot's wheel with both hands and settled my feet against the rudder pedals. Under his mustache, Anza kept muttering something, numbers it sounded like, counting backwards from 20 in a mixture of Spanish, English, and Yaqui. As we neared the cliff, the wingstruts began to creak and groan. The winch operators flattened themselves against the ground, arms and legs asprawl like flies under pressure of an inexorable swatter. With a shudder that ripped from cockpit to tail, the glider heaved off the strip, buoyed by a stiff breeze sweeping over the cliff. The poultry grew deathly silent, except for a terrified hen that cackled insanely. The ground fell away, plunging hundreds of feet into a quarry of jagged rocks. *"Now!"* Anza hissed, scattering mustache hairs against his taut knuckles. I pulled back on the wheel with all my might and jammed my feet against the pedals. The nose tipped up, and with a final shudder the glider soared out into space.

The rejoicing was universal. The poultry clucked and gobbled, the passengers grinned and exchanged handshakes. Tension eased from my body in a bubbling stream that oozed out my boots and dripped onto the cockpit floor. After leveling off at 3,000 feet over the Borrego Valley, Anza collected the cyanide caps and deposited them in a pill jar. "For the next trip," he said with a wink.

He looked every inch the veteran of the Hump, which he was not. Forty years old, fluent in a half-dozen languages, blessed with a personality that could charm the rust off a boiler, he was a natural flyer, even though he didn't possess a pilot's license. "I'm strictly a lighter-than-air bug," he explained. "Motors give me a headache and jets scare me shitless. I like the silence rushing around me, the breeze through the struts. No reason why you can't have both locomotion and serenity."

Over the little village of Temecula we sailed, the passengers looking eagerly out the wide glider windows. From a range of mountains to our port side, the eye of the Palomar telescope tracked us carefully, observing every feature and blemish on the old, war-surplus aircraft. Beautiful green fields unfolded under the glider, cultivated by patient, loving hands, and dotted with ponds and stands of eucalyptus trees, beneath which nestled adobe houses and looping corrals. An old Gene Autry number crackled over the two-way radio, raising a lump in the throat of the most grizzled *campesino* amongst us. To the west, low foothills swept up in soft, swelling blocks to the jagged rim of the coastal range. The scene was golden California at its finest, a cornucopia of vegetable gardens and grapefruit orchards, grazing land and tangled chaparral—lush, fertile, paradisaical.

Past Temecula, running north-south, lay the asphalt barrier of Interstate 15, connecting San Diego with San Bernadino. Traffic snarled up and down the lanes, an interminable parade of pickups, produce trucks, semis, sports cars, commuters, limousines, recreation vehicles, vans. Curling out from the Interstate in ugly brown cankers were developments and bedroom communities, whorls and tentacles of featureless housing, geometrically exact but inadequately spaced, an unchecked spillover from the urban centers fifty miles away, oozing like dirty sludge into unspoiled valleys and secret canyons. At the highway we turned south, Anza leaning hard against the wheel and pumping the left rudder, the glider moaning and shuddering under the strain. Between a pair of bald peaks we cruised, riding the crest of a salt-laden swell. Over the pass the land cascaded toward the ocean in a series of terraced descents, like gigantic paving stones sunk progressively deeper into the coastal slope and mantled with orchards and vineyards. In a narrow ravine just east of Oceanside was a shabby racetrack and ramshackled stables. Further on, through the mist brewing off the surf, glistened the pearly sepulchre of the Mission San Luis Rey.

Over Escondido an appalling orange cloud greeted us, hard evidence of big-city smog. Anza skirted it to the north, but close enough to collect a scummy residue like potato grease on the wings and struts. Below, the Interstate vanished into a multilayered cloverleaf that sent tributaries whirling in every direction. Northwest of Escondido, a police helicopter, keeping tabs on the traffic, buzzed alongside like a wasp. Two F-4 Phantoms from the Naval base at El Torreon streaked overhead, rocking the glider in their sonic wash.

The distance was only eighty miles as the condor flies, but it took all afternoon to reach the bluffs behind La Jolla. The passage of time was as effortless as an afternoon spent lolling on a park bench. Coffee was served, with peach cobbler and brandy, followed by cheroots, hand-rolled by pregnant teenagers in Jalisco and wrapped with a leaf flavored strongly of chicory. Past Escondido a chicken became hysterical and had to be silenced. With a Swiss Army knife the owner snapped

67

off the head and shook the spurting neck around the cabin like a garden hose. Drenched in blood, the passengers applauded ecstatically and contributed a few coins apiece to compensate for the loss.

As the sun sank over the hills, the cabin lights came on, more brandy was decanted, fresh cigars handed out, and one by one, each passenger stepped forth as if onto a softly lit stage and sang a song or related a story of his or her life. Some told of fortunes earned and squandered, others of messy love affairs, unhappy marriages, illicit trysts in empty barns and abandoned cafés. Still others told of ungrateful children, of babies birthed and buried, of adolescence aflame with lust, of their own childhoods to the east and south, filled with misery and love, squalor and affection. Still others descanted upon their experiences in war, the savor of battle, the implacable sting of a bullet, the numbing fear that reduced them to knots of quivering flesh. After they had finished, Anza, in a rolling baritone capped by high-C crescendos, recounted his early days as an altar boy in the old mission village of Caborca, in Sonora, where he and his chums used to get drunk on communion wine and take turns buggering the padre.

One day when he was around thirteen, he experienced a most unusual sensation. The mission stood on the edge of town, at the end of a little plaza. Behind it was nothing but open desert, dotted with saguaro cactus and bleak volcanic rock. Built in the 18th century of Moorish design, it boasted a minaretlike bell tower, circular windows, and walls fashioned from slabs of rock salt. One dazzling day in mid-June, with the sun pumping light into every cranny, young Anza strode boldly across the plaza and straight through the stark mission walls and out the other side.

"It was a little like dying," he said in a rapt whisper, clearly audible in the noiseless glider: "I saw and heard nothing but white. It was like standing in the center of a cataract, opaque and annealed, a vision totally contained within the dimensions of itself. Immediately my body left me, and I felt no heaviness, no gravitational connection with the earth. I was suspended in a translucent solution of pure ecstasy, and with every passing second I could feel the walls around me grow thicker and more impermeable. It was like being trapped inside a force that is independent of all other forces around it, an autonomous state of being contingent on no other laws than those of its own devising...."

"And you, a good Catholic, with that effort became a blasphemer," said a rancher from Hemet.

"You challenged God's will," said another.

"You desecrated the body of the Mother Church," said another.

"You flaunted the physical laws of the universe."

"Like so many others," said the rancher, indicating the tangerine pall blanketing the lights of Escondido.

"But how did you escape?" I said.

"I was wearing spurs," the pilot explained, "with fiery rowls, an heirloom of my illustrious ancestor, Captain Juan Bautista de Anza, first explorer and colonizer of these parts. When I felt the shell around me growing thicker, I kicked my heels and slapped my thighs and broke out into the blinding air of the desert. For a minute everything was so stark and brilliant I thought I was still back inside. Then the heat struck me and I knew I was free."

"A miracle!"

"Fantastic!"

"Incredible!"

"Since that time I have never been without them," said Anza. "I sleep with them under the pillow."

As the lights of La Jolla came into view, sprinkled along the bluffs between the coastal freeway and the beach, an atmosphere of contentment and well-being suffused the cabin. More cigars were fired, brandy poured, compliments extended, anecdotes swapped. Under the seats and from on top of the cushions, the hens and geese and ducks and turkeys clucked softly to one another.

The pleasant feeling in my bowels evaporated as I stared down at the rudder pedals. "But... you're not wearing them now!" I whispered, gaping at Anza's spurless boots tucked carefully under the pilot's seat.

"Hush, Sweetcheeks," he cautioned, pressing a finger against his lips and turning deathly pale. "Don't let the others know."

3.

Over the bluffs we soared, passing houses tucked in the folds, Anza peering ahead toward the beach. It was almost dark, with only a smoldering red glow out on the horizon to indicate the vanished sun. To our left, rolling along a carpet of low hills, were the lights of La Jolla. Over Cardiff, a small village crowded right down to the edge of the sand, we banked to the left and angling away from the lights, out toward the surf, began our descent. The cabin lights went off, the brandy was returned to the cupboard, cigars were extinguished. The passengers squared around in their seats, belted themselves in, and

70

planted their feet firmly on the floor. Gulls drifted between the wing struts, mewing nastily. Cardiff dropped behind; leaning out, I could see the phosphorescent caps of the great Pacific breakers dashing toward shore and hear their reverberant booming.

A hundred feet off the sand, an ocean gust scooped under the right wing and threw us off course in the direction of the coastal highway. Tromping the rudders, I yanked the wheel over, following Anza's direction and partially corrected the glider's drift. We were steering for a line of oil drums running parallel to the surf which were flickering like matchsticks, illuminating the beach in a caramel glow.

Working swiftly, Anza tried to wrestle the craft over on a path to the right of the barrels, between them and the surf, but the wind wheeling in off the waves was too strong, and the craft kept veering to the other side. Just behind the oil drums was an assortment of beach paraphernalia—tents, cabanas, rowboats, lifeguard stands. Throwing his body against the wheel, Anza aimed the glider toward a narrow strip between the oil drums and beach gear, but not even his considerable skills were enough to thread that needle. The left wingtip struck a lifeguard stand, and the craft wobbled to earth like a wounded albatross. A second later the nose struck the beach, throwing up sheets of wet sand. The impact knocked over an oil drum, spilling fiery kerosene. Around we spun in a grinding circle, chicken feathers clouding the cabin as if a pillow had been ripped open. Around in the wet, heavy sand we spun again, snapping wing struts and ailerons. My left hand smashed against the control board, breaking a dial and opening a deep gash. Once more we twisted around, wiping out another

71

lifeguard stand, with poultry squawking, people screaming, the glider cracking and groaning like a frigate in a hurricane, before shuddering to a halt.

An uneasy silence numbed the interior. A second later a storm of clucks and shrieks broke loose. The rancher from Hemet flung open the emergency hatch and began throwing chickens onto the sand. Then he tumbled out headfirst and crawled off. Pressing my bleeding hand against my chest, I unclasped the belt and somersaulted backward over the seat and began hurling passengers and poultry out the hatch. Shrieks, yells, roars, groans, curses, drowned out my pleas for sanity and order. The cabin was a mess: blood, feathers, fruit, vegetables were scattered everywhere; seats were ripped, windows smashed, brandy spilled, cigars squashed. With all the passengers out, I turned to Anza, only to find him slumped over the wheel, his chest punctured by a wingstrut which had pierced the glider's flimsy canvas hide, wounding him fatally.

A writer of detective fiction, an amiable man in tweeds, helped me pull the body from the cockpit. He had been wandering along the beach, formulating the plot for his next thriller, when the glider crashed. The weightlessness Anza experienced walking through the mission at Caborca was revenged upon him at death. Slumped over the wheel, a spar poking from his chest, he weighed a ton, he weighed more than a truckload of elephants. The mystery writer and I couldn't budge him. "I didn't think death was that heavy," the writer remarked in a faint Devonshire accent. Fortunately a gang of surfers, muscular young men, wandered up and helped us haul the body out of the cockpit and onto the sand. A grief-stricken passenger—a distant cousin of

72

Anza's—beheaded a rooster and dusted the dead man's face with blood. After plucking the feathers, the cousin arranged a curly tiara in Anza's hair and spoke a few words of Yaqui. In the pilot's wallet we found a laminated card instructing TO WHOM IT MAY CONCERN to dispose of his body by fire immediately upon death.

We had to act fast before the police arrived with their flashlights and brutal questions. With the surfers' help, we lifted Anza's body back into the glider and stretched it on the floor. Kerosene from the oil drums was slopped over the fuselage and wings. A match was struck and with a loud whump! the craft went up in flames. In a few minutes the wings dissolved and the taut hide over the fuselage peeled away revealing a ribbed interior and the remains of Captain Anza. The mystery writer took lavish notes; the surfers gallivanted around the burning hulk, chanting hymns to King Kamehameha, the great Sandwich Island warrior. Finally the police arrived, but there was little they could do except take everybody's name. Toward dawn, the rubble cooled off enough so we could scoop the ashes into a grocery sack, and we walked along the waterfront scattering them on bougainvillea and oleanders.

A surfer named Ricky took me to his cottage up in the hills. My hand throbbed miserably, and I had lost a lot of blood. High on a brown hill, facing the ocean, sat Ricky's house, a modest clapboard dwelling draped with nets woven from kelp, seaweed, and jellyfish tentacles. Surfboards lined the walls, of varying sizes and shapes, some greased with pitch from the rare Torrey pine, others with marmalade and candle wax. The most spectacular—long as a canoe and decorated with Polynesian fetish symbols—had the spine of a hammerhead shark for a keel. Ricky's girlfriend and an older woman named Rae helped me into the kitchen. Their touch was gentle, and their moist skin exuded the unmistakable scent of honeysuckle. At the table they bathed my hand in well water and wrapped the wound between two slices of cactus pulp cored out of a prickly stalk of the *cardón*. The cut throbbed like a jackhammer, and I tried to be brave, but the tears rolled helplessly down my cheeks. Rae brewed a pot of *yerba del pasmo* tea and served it in a shallow bowl laced with honey. A few sips and I was gone. Who were these creatures clad in breech-clouts, with their marvelous healing smiles? Before I could find out, I collapsed in the hammock strung across the back porch and sank into oblivion.

4.

I slept all the next day. When I woke up, Rae was sitting beside me, balming my forehead and fanning the flies away with a flipper from a scuba outfit. A tall, stately woman around fifty years of age, with large bones, long limbs, and drooping breasts, she reminded me a lot of Hetty. Her wide gray eyes, pointed nose, and high sloping forehead were very much like Hetty's. Lying in the hammock, sipping tea and munching rice cakes, I followed her avidly with my eyes as she slipped into the kitchen, crossed the living room, and swung back out on the porch. She walked with a rolling, seaman's gait, her toes outpointed, the soles of her big feet making a soft flopping sound on the floorboards, the flesh on her thighs shimmering like suet in a bird feeder. Her voice was husky, a terse bronchial rasp, a good deal harsher

74

than Hetty's, but with the same note of authority and intelligence.

My clothing had been removed and replaced by a soft, onepiece garment. My hand still hurt, but when Rae unwrapped the bandage I was astonished to discover that the cut had closed and the swelling gone down considerably. The wound was white and pulpy as insect larvae, and looked well on the way to healing. Slicing open a fresh *cardón*, she carved out two hunks and squeezed them against my hand, then bound the whole thing with a cloth and a strip of adhesive.

After devouring a bowl of abalone and oyster stew, I gimped around the house. Instruments cluttered the rooms—strange, grotesque instruments: kelp horns and gourd rattles, bull roarers and nose flutes, fingerdrums and spiritcatchers, mouthbows and water chimes, seed-pod shakers and konch shells, signal flutes and bird whistles, calabash horns and walking marimbas. The living room was taken up by a driftwood harmonium powered by a whale's bladder that produced a deep, resonant groan that sounded as if it came all the way from the depths of the Marianas Trench.

"Ricky and I are working on a new instrument," Rae said, as she settled on the floor beside the hammock: "One that will reproduce the sound a surfer hears as he shoots through the tube. I don't surf, so I don't know what that sound is. Ricky says it's a high-pitched squeal, steady and piercing as a siren, only warmer and fuller, much warmer and fuller. He thinks it's like the sound those goddesses made when they tempted Ulysses as he sailed through the Straits of Chronos. A shrill, insistent sound, yet seductive and enchanting. He says that when you're getting tubed the sound is so hypnotic you can

75

lose control of your faculties and get wiped out before you reach the end. That's the kind of sound we're trying to reproduce."

I stared at her, fascinated.

"During all the years he's been surfing, Ricky's heard the sound only three times—once off Baja, once off Oahu, and once off Big Rock here in La Jolla. Hearing the sound is an incandescent experience, he says. You shed your body and become like a bolt of light, an erg of pure energy, trapped inside the tube, yet outside it, an elemental life force like the sea or the wind. And the only way you can achieve this phenomenon is to place yourself in a position of extreme jeopardy."

"What... uh... materials will you make this instrument out of?"

"Ricky. Himself."

"Pardon?"

"He has heard the sound, so the sound is still inside him. It has made a permanent impression on his nerve endings and brain cells. Working together, we have already been able to approximate the sound, at least the one he described to me. When he heard it on the tape I made of his voice, he said it was very close to the sound he heard in his head as he was getting tubed off Big Rock. Ricky will be the instrument. You'll see when he gets home, later, from the beach."

Leo's voice suddenly chattered in my ear, harsh and scolding. I shook my head and took a sip of tea.

"The sound has definite salutary powers," continued Rae, shifting around on the floor and cradling her big breasts in the crook of her elbows. "It can stop a burglar in his tracks. Banks and stores could use it as an alarm. Doctors could use it to anesthetize patients. For spacepersons on long voyages, it could reduce their pulse rate and respiration to that of a hibernating bear. With a bit more frequency, it could be used as an aphrodisiac for impotent men. For the old and incurably ill, it could be used as a device for euthanasia."

"Pretty strong sound."

"Yes, but there's an even stronger one." Her face reddened with enthusiasm and her eyes grew very bright.

"What's that?"

"Inside a woman's vagina, in front of the cervix, there's an appendage, a tough little piece of gristle which, when placed in the proper amplifier, makes a fantastic tweeter. I once saw one in a museum in Cuzco. I've never heard the sound, but I'm told there's nothing like it, that it's the most powerful aural force ever devised, stronger than Jerico's trumpet or the horns of Milton's angels. It can shatter rock and level cities. The Incas used it against their enemies to extend their power up and down the west coast of South America. They tried it against the Spaniards, but the Spaniards were immune. The European ear cannot properly detect the pitch, and so the effect was lost on them. The sound was merely irritating and made them fight harder."

"Do all women have this ... tweeter?"

"Of course not. Some are more gifted than others. But only in the incubator of the vagina could such an appendage take root. Men are incapable of conceiving such an apparatus."

"How do you know if you have this... talent?" I asked.

"It's a feeling you get at first. You get it a few years after you enter puberty, after your body adjusts to all the changes of adolescence and womanhood. You feel a certain power, totally unrelated to sex, a kind of verbal or vocal power that enables you to hum and talk very loudly. You get the feeling that with the strength of your voice alone you could blow down trees or sweep the water out of a lake. That's when you start talking softly and watching carefully what you say in order to protect and preserve the power. It's too extraordinary to waste on an unworthy object."

"Do you have this power inside you?"

"Yes. I was thirteen years old when I realized it."

"Is it . . . bothered at all when you have intercourse?"

"No. A man can sometimes feel it with his penis, but no matter how hard he pumps he can't harm it."

She looked at me carefully for a moment, running her gray eyes back and forth across my face. Then she stood up and unraveled the breechclout from her waist. I was lying in the hammock, with my wounded hand pillowed on a towel. She stepped up next to me, and took my good hand and placed it on her crotch. "Put your finger up there," she said, "and you can almost certainly feel it."

I did, and, after poking around a bit, finally located the tweeter in front of her cervix. It was very far up—in order to really see it I would have to remove it surgically. My probing seemed to have no effect; Rae stared down at me calmly, telling me where to touch, a placid expression on her face. I felt like a man standing in front of a full closet pawing through the racks looking for something to wear.

Finally, she stepped back and put her breechclout back on. "I've never told anyone about it before," she confessed. "Not even when I was married. My gynecologist knows, but she has one too, so my secret is safe."

"Why have you told me then?"

"Because there's something in your face that tells me you are trustworthy," she replied. "Your face is very gentle and serene; it's the kind of face that people want to confess things to. It's a very understanding face, a sensitive face. From what you've told me, I don't think you're interested in expropriating other people's power."

"I hope I'm never in a position where I have to resort to that."

"If the message is waiting for you inside the beard, like you've been told, then all you have to do is walk up and stick your hand inside."

"I hope it's that simple."

5.

I fell asleep again before Ricky got home, a restless, brooding sleep highlighted by an incoherent dream featuring vocalist Jerry Vale and the pioneer French aviator Louis Blériot. Blériot was piloting his rickety monoplane upside down over the choppy waters of the English Channel. Ahead loomed the ghostly white cliffs of Dover, shrouded in fog and mist, looking like a phalanx of icebergs drifting down from the Arctic. Standing on one of the cliffs, arms extended, head cocked to one side in classic Las Vegas style, was Jerry Vale, crooning with nasal panache the lyrics to the sentimental favorite, "In Amorata." His voice acted like a sonar beam, beckoning to the aircraft, actually pulling it forward along the line of an invisible lanyard. Just before the craft reached the cliffs, Jerry hit the final notes of the tune and faded from view to the swishing sound of a curtain and peals of thunderous applause. The aircraft faltered, the motor spluttered. Hanging upside down in the straps, Blériot tried valiantly to righten the ship but his hands had fused into a solid mass and he couldn't grasp hold of the stick. Fortunately, I woke up before the aircraft hit the cliff.

I was on the floor, on my side, my cheek pressed against the porch boards, one foot caught in the hammock. Through the door, I saw Ricky sitting in a straight-backed chair in the middle of the kitchen. Rae stood behind him, squeezing his fudgy nipples between her fingers. Ricky's mouth was open and from his lips curdled a funny cry that rose higher and higher. The sound wasn't especially loud but it was piercing, a high-pitched, fibrillating quiver that drilled through my brain like a needle. Working his nipples like radio dials, Rae slowly amplified Ricky's voice. Up and up it went, Ricky pausing only to gulp more air before opening his mouth wider to emit a powerful shriek that rattled the kitchen windows and rippled the leaves outside on the silk oak.

I tore off the tunic Rae had wrapped me in and staggered over to the clothesline where my shirt and trousers hung. Ricky's girlfriend sat on the steps leading down to the yard, a dazed look gilding her features. Her lips parted as though she wanted to say something, but nothing came out and all she could manage was a feeble wave. Clumsily, I pulled my boots on. Lacing them took an eternity. My fingers felt so stiff I could barely manage to tie a knot. My duffel was in the kitchen. With a great effort, dragging myself along the floor like a wounded animal, I crawled in and retrieved it. Ricky's head was thrown back, cushioned against Rae's breasts, and his mouth was open and he was howling with all his might.

80

Rae played his nipples with the skill of an acoustical engineer, eliciting a louder wail with every twist. Down the steps I stumbled, nodding drunkenly to the girl and hitting the yard like a bag of sand. For the longest time I lay there, feeling nothing, thinking nothing, until a voice inside my head exhorted me to get up . . . *get up* . . . GET UP. On my feet at last, I lurched against the silk oak, bounced off, and staggered out into the street.

A lingering twilight, shot through with sour yellow streaks, hung over the trees. Ricky's voice hailed down the street, loud and inexhaustible, slowing the procession of elderly couples, the flight of birds from tree to tree. My breath grew labored and rasping, my legs felt like lead, an oppressive weight pushed me slowly to the sidewalk beside a lawn trimmed with marigolds. On the grass stood a man, wearing cut-offs and T-shirt, holding a hose. Water trickled out the nozzle; smoke curled sluggishly from the cigar in his mouth. He stood motionless, head tilted, eyes staring, frozen in a posture of sculpted rigidity.

Curled up in a fetal position, with my hands over my ears, I would have remained there forever, if it hadn't been for the skateboard. Overturned on the sidewalk a few feet away, abandoned, most likely, by some kid called into supper (I could imagine him now, sitting at the table, his fork hanging in space between his plate and half-opened mouth). Gritting my teeth, I crawled over and with a tremendous effort righted the board and shoved it into the street. Cushioning my body with the duffel, I flopped facedown and gave a push with my foot. The board started out at a crawl, bumping over the uneven surface. Despite the tug of gravity and well-greased wheels, the skateboard inched slowly down a precipitous hill. Near the bottom it picked up momentum, and a second later I went sailing through an intersection, fortunately empty of cars, and banged to a halt beside a sewer.

I found I had returned to the beach where Anza's glider had crashed. I stood up, shook myself all over, and walked quickly past the smoldering remains. The lifeguard stand had been replaced, and a greasy splotch marked the sand where the oil drums had been knocked over. Lost in thought, ambling along the edge of the surf, flannel trousers rolled up to his knees, was the writer of detective fiction. "You again," he growled in a soft, clipped voice.

"Pardon me, but can you tell me how to get to Mexico? I need to get to Mexico right away."

"Down the beach another mile is a railway depot."

"Is it open?"

"It's always open. A train leaves for the border every hour or so. So many people willing to give up everything they've achieved to enter the unknown." His round face, banded with tortoise-shell glasses, registered intense disapproval.

"That's their business."

"Nothing down there you're going to find that's any different from up here," he scowled. "You young people are all alike. You think that by following every new impulse you can discover a new direction. There are no new directions; there's only one, and that leads to you know where. The key is to properly order and modulate your flight along its path."

"There are paths leading everywhere," I objected. "There are directions pointing everywhere... up... down... around... outside... inside... over...

above. The key is to inhabit a space that offers the most possibilities."

"That's chaos you're talking about, young man, and people have no business inhabiting a space they can't make sense out of let alone order to suit their own tastes. You young people ought to pay more attention to plot instead of letting your noses lead you where they will."

"Yes, sir... well, sir... I've got to be going."

"Plot is what makes the reader turn the page," he declared, gesturing vehemently with the stem of his pipe. "You young people don't want to plot or chart anything. You think by sprinkling words on a page you can hold a reader's attention. Rubbish. You have to be more precise than that. Structure is not achieved by accident; it is deliberately and carefully created. You ought to be aware of that; you look like an intelligent fellow. It is into the mold of structure that you pour the life-giving elements of a story... character, dialogue, description. You don't smear them randomly across a page like peanut butter! There's a great deal of choice and selection involved!"

As I walked off, I saw him wade into the surf and shout his arguments defiantly to the plunging sea.

CHAPTER V

The club car was crowded with people. Stepping around water skis, surfboards, and life vests, I reached the bar and ordered a bottle of Double-X. Oddly enough, the air was smoke-free. A notice on the wall said that anyone lighting up a cigarette was subject to verbal abuse or a glass of water thrown in the face. Strong, masculine voices rang off the walls and ceiling, drowning out all whispers of intrigue. This was a public place, and all concerns, whether spoken or intimated, had to be made in a loud, declarative fashion. As a result, the air was charged with assertive voices; it was like standing in a ring with a dozen boxers throwing punches at your head. The slick Art Deco interior reflected a cool and polished vitality, but the sound of the voices did not stick to the surfaces. If the train stopped and everybody got off, the interior would resound with no echoes or reverberations, it would merely be another empty, unmarked space.

A chair opened up at a nearby table into which I slipped, stuffing my duffel between my legs. A man about forty shared it, handsomely dressed in pleated trousers and a white cashmere tennis sweather, edged with blue piping. A paperback extolling the nutritional wonders of papaya lay cover up across a clean ash tray.

Next to it, balanced with pristine elegance, stood a carafe of white wine. "Heading south?" he murmured.

"Yes. Enseñada."

"Nice town." Tapered fingers curled around the neck of the carafe and tipped more wine into a long-stemmed glass. "Plan to fish?"

"No... no... I have a... a prescription to fill."

He looked at me attentively. Attractive face, bronzed by the sun, firm jaw, glimmering teeth, smooth forehead, wincing Roy Rogers eyes.

"Good place for that. Enseñada has a cure for most everything."

I downed my Double-X and ordered another. The waiter looked woefully out of place amid these carefully coiffured people. He wore a seedy white jacket stained with food, and coarse woolen trousers with bulky cuffs rolled up over his ankles.

"Let me get this," the fellow said, peeling a five-spot off a money clip branded with his initials. "I'm celebrating something."

"Double-X!" I said.

"Coming up!" the waiter cried.

"You know where I was a year ago at this time?" the man asked me.

"No, where?"

"In a clinic getting cured of a vile disease known as the Evtuffel Syndrome."

I spit a mouthful of beer on the arm of the waiter who was leaning over making change. "Pardon... pardon," I gasped.

"No worry," the waiter said. "Spitting beer is an act of love."

"A really trashy affliction," continued the man in the

86

tennis sweater. "Characterized by a stiffening of the skin, a tortoiselike hardening of the pores. Caused primarily by stress. I contracted a real dose. I looked like an armadillo. You could bounce an arrow off my chest."

"How did you get rid of it?"

"There's a clinic in Brentwood run by a doctor named Bilkstrode. He has another place in Palm Springs. I checked in on a Monday, and by Thursday my skin was normal again. An ordeal, but it was worth it."

The waiter hovered at my elbow (ostensibly polishing the arm of my chair) but, really, listening to our conversation.

"It's a very popular clinic. They've got people backed up eight and nine months waiting to get in. They're opening a new branch in Santa Monica and another in Laguna Beach. I'm negotiating for an option to buy a chunk of stock."

"That good a prospect, eh?" said the waiter.

"Better. The way the market is today? Real estate is the best investment you can make, pharmaceuticals next. Stress, and how to cope with it, will soon be third. I own a string of health-food bars along the coast from Coronado to Santa Barbara. Yucca-Manna, International. We have outlets in Ensenada and Santa Rosalia. Heard of us?"

I shook my head.

"We're coming. Another year and we'll go public. If you've got some loose change in a drawer and want a speedy, bullish return, give us a try. Here's my card."

Embossed lettering beneath a swirling yucca blossom logo read: A. STANTON TURNER, PRESIDENT & CHAIRMAN OF THE BOARD.

The waiter took a bite out of the corner and filed it

away under his greasy jacket.

"This Bilkstrode is a genius. Ever heard of him?"

"I think so . . ."

"Probably the foremost cosmetician in the world. He can do more with the human skin than the entire make-up department at Paramount. A year ago you wouldn't have recognized me. I was bloated, my skin was green, my voice had a funny click to it. In four days Bilkstrode erased all that. What a wizard! He took a hideous creature and made him, may I say immodestly, into a pretty good-looking guy. I'm eternally indebted. That's why I want to buy all the shares I can get my hands on. Bilkstrode Enterprises is a comer. Like Yucca-Manna, International. People are health and body-conscious today, more than ever before, and not just here in California either. Everywhere. People don't want to be ugly anymore; they want to look healthy and natural. That scruffy, hippie look of the sixties is passé. People want to look rich. You know how rich people always look strong and pink-cheeked and vibrant? Well, that's the way people want to look. And that's what Bilkstrode and I can give them."

"What about recurrence?" I said.

"Of the Evtuffel Syndrome? Oh, high, very high. Around 75 percent, I was told. Which makes the potential for business even better. If I keep going at my present rate, I should be showing fresh symptoms in another eight or nine months. Next year at this time I should be in the hospital for another cure."

"Why don't you stop what you're doing?"

"And let another hustler beat me to the tape? We're talking Big Bucks, ducky, Big Bucks. Health foods and cosmetic surgery are the comers on the American economic scene. It's not the record business anymore, the oil boys put the quietus on that. Stress is here to stay. For sure. Your average bloke isn't going to escape it unless he moves to a ghost town in Nevada. Been to Los Angeles lately? Even if the Feds handed out free emission-control devices, people wouldn't use them. They're locked into their gadgets and conveniences and can't be pried out of them on threat of death. LA will look and smell like it does a hundred years from today. People aren't interested in making changes. So long as they look and feel good, they don't care how bad the air is. Cosmetology is the new super industry. It's a comer. So don't talk to me about solutions. Without pollution, there's no cosmetology. That's why I believe in both the cause and the cure. They're good for business."

2.

Next morning we reached the border, an electric fence topped with barbed wire stretching from the ocean into the mountains. Behind us, to the north and west, lay San Diego, basking like a bed of mussels in the feeble sun. The distance from La Jolla to the border was only fifty miles as the seagull soars; we should have been there in an hour, but repeated strikes, crew walkouts, protestors on the tracks, a bridge destroyed by terrorists, the birth of quintuplets in the parlor car, a gun battle between rival cocaine dealers, a landslide south of Chula Vista, a flash flood east of San Ysidro, a violent electrical storm that knocked out power for six hours, an attempted heist by a band of Mexican guerillas, and a minor tremor that split the tracks southeast of Imperial Beach held us up. We

89

didn't reach the border until 7 o'clock the next morning, twelve hours after I got on in La Jolla. Time was slipping away like a tarantula easing down a dry creek bed. It was Wednesday morning... only five days to go.

A catwalk arching up to a wooden platform high over the wire fence marked the entry way. On top stood four guards—two U.S. Customs officials and two Mexicans. I combed through my duffel and eliminated all suspicious sticks and twigs. The polished abalone whistle given me by the Witiki squaw I put carefully in my front pocket. Lining the approach to the platform was a gauntlet of stalls advertising food, liquid refreshment, passport photographs, forged entry visas, insurance packages, and sightseeing tours.

"Hey, buddy," a vendor called. "Over here. I got something for you." A stooped, spindly man with a snub nose like a koala bear and a hat woven of manzanita leaves. "Going into Mexico?"

"Enseñada."

"You'll need this." He held up a ring with a wide band.

"No souvenirs, please."

"This isn't that kind of ring," he explained. "This is a special *turista* device, in case you get the *turista*."

"What's it do?"

"It's a special noncorrosive device that fits right into your asshole. If you get the green shits, you can fire away without wearing your asshole to a pulp. After shitting, all you have to do is slip it out and rinse it off and shove it back in. Believe me, it saves a lot of wear and tear."

"No thanks."

"You'll regret it. Burning asshole is one of the worst agonies known to man."

"I have a cast-iron stomach."

90

"Don't say that! It's bad luck! When your asshole catches fire and you're looking for a well to plop it in, you'll remember me. They got creepy crawlies down there you can't believe. You can suck food through a straw from a sanitized carton flown all the way from Portland, and you'll still pick up the little varmints. They're in the air. Mexico is a cruel, vindictive place."

"I'm traveling in peace as a friend," I said. "I mean no harm to anyone."

"How about a cork then? Got a special deal, velvet wrapped, guaranteed to plug you up for ten days no matter how loudly your bowels complain. Cost you a buck."

3.

The funicular chugged up the steep bluff, gears gnashing, passengers tittering as the vehicle grated over a rusty spot on the tracks. Below lay Tijuana, smoldering like a rubbish heap, throwing up columns of gritty smoke. Beneath the pall flickered innumerable fires. Tiny figures darted in and out of the rubble. A ghastly stench—a composite of trash, chemicals, burning rubber, and feces—stung our nostrils. Handkerchiefs appeared, eyes filled with tears, faces turned away from the scene. "My God," a young girl whispered, "who would want to go there?"

"You'd be surprised," said a voice. "Underneath that offal lies a fortune in buried treasure."

"But it's so... appalling!"

"Tijuana is the most misunderstood place in the world. But, then, that's the way the Mexicans want it."

91

It was the waiter from the club car. He had followed us across the catwalk into Mexico wearing clumsy sabots, a tufted kepi, and carrying a canvas bag marked LAKERS. A raincoat with a tattered hem hung to his ankles. In the morning light, the cracks and seams in his leathery face were caulked with grime and bacon grease. His watery blue eyes shifted with alcoholic nervousness above the promonotory of a blunt, pugilist's nose. So successful was this disguise that the other passengers shied out of reach like spooked horses against the rim of a corral.

"The Mexicans have arranged it this way," he explained as the funicular bumped to a halt at the top of the bluff. "Tijuana is their prize heap. Every pimp, shyster, and con artist in western Mexico scavenges off fat American tourists down there. Americans have a preconception of Mexico anyway—dirty, smelly, dishonest. Tijuana fulfills that preconception. Only the hardiest, the most disinterested, the best travelers—yourselves, I presume—will venture further south. The Mexicans are a proud, sensitive people, and they do not wish to be plagued with riffraff. Underneath that inferno down there they have planted scores of gold nuggets calculated to spark the greed in the heart of the most parsimonious gringo. Most visitors are willing to put up with the smoke and the smell just to try and find those goodies. It's a real adventure for them and satisfies whatever desire they have to be in a foreign country. They get robbed, they get beaten up, they get thrown in jail. The experience intensifies an already rampant xenophobia and sends them scrambling for the border, never to return. Which is precisely what the Mexican government wants."

At the top, the passengers disembarked and went their separate ways. The majority started down the weedy

92

path that wound over a series of smoothly rounded hills toward the bullring sitting on the beach a couple of miles away. Open at the top, with seats sloping in tiers to a blood-red ring, it resembled a flying saucer parked sedately on the sand.

There were four of us heading for Enseñada: the waiter, myself, and a young newlywed couple from Ventura. Their names were Alicia and Brad, or Deidre and Kent, or Melanie and Lance . . . I didn't catch which. The girl's nipples glowed through her white blouse like bicycle reflectors. Her skin was flawless, her hips and crotch snugly corseted in a pair of jeans. They both wore dark Polaroid glasses, which accentuated their smooth, chiseled features. The girl's lipstick matched the polish of her manicured nails. The boy sported a gold ring on his left pinky that glittered like a canary's tongue.

Down the ridge we proceeded into a shallow ravine with a corral where we selected our horses for the journey to Enseñada. I chose an appaloosa, the couple picked a pair of palominos, while the waiter, leaping on and off half a dozen, finally settled on a sturdy buckskin. Saddled up, with an escort of five sombreroed *vaqueros*, we picked our way southeast through a narrow defile into the first of the great interior valleys of Lower California.

To the west, over the mountains, there was a four-lane highway, which we avoided. It was a toll road, heavily patrolled by a fiendish military cadre culled from the ranks of the most reactionary Latin-American republics and accorded this spot by international decree in hopes they might eventually kill each other off. Officered by squint-eyed thugs from Nicaragua, Colombia, and Chile, the cadre took delight in machine-gunning tourists and preying like rapacious jackals upon the local

93

population. Hardly a desirable stretch, by any means, despite its breathtaking beauty. You either had to drive it at breakneck speed, at night, with no lights, or pay an outrageous fee for an escort that usually ended up gunning you down. To complicate matters, destroyers from the Mexican Navy periodically shelled the road to harass the cutthroats and disrupt their operations. Enseñada was, thankfully, inaccessible to them—its magic and power were too strong to overcome, and every attempt to subdue it had been successfully repelled. This was true of the interior valleys as well, where the *campesinos* put up a stiff resistance. If a jeep or truck strayed over the coast range, it was promptly ambushed and the intruders butchered. It was a dirty, savage conflict along the littoral of a stunning coastline, littered with the bones of wrecked freighters, over which swarmed flocks of hungry pelicans... a place of sumptuous natural beauty, tragically reduced by politics to a void, a killing zone.

The waiter gave me this information. His name was Robert Lacaud, Jr., and he declared he was the last of the hobos, a creature who picked up information on the wing as easily as a nighthawk does insects under a street lamp.

As the afternoon wore on, blisters the size of half-dollars began to rise on my soft ass. I shifted awkwardly from cheek to cheek, much to the amusement of Lacaud who lolled easily in the saddle as if he'd been born to it. The young couple rode the same horse, the girl straddling the boy's lap, locked in a hungry embrace. The *vaqueros* snickered approvingly and rolled enormous spliffs out of cornsilks which they inhaled in chest-swelling draughts.

It took most of the afternoon to negotiate the first

94

valley. Rainclouds crept over the mountains in dark bunches, wetting the trail with a slick drizzle. A rocky stream gushed alongside. At the little village of El Testarazo, we paused for a drink and a bite of tortilla. The inhabitants gathered around curiously, young boys and girls dressed in sackcloth and *huaraches*, old women with flour on their fingers, men with hoes and rakes, their feet sticky with mud. Lacaud came prepared, his saddlebags stuffed with tape recorders and pocket calculators, which he traded for a suit of tanned leather, tasseled with buckskin and a *sombrero vaqueteado*, fringed with palm leaves and covered with deerskin. The transformation was astonishing—from a seedy itinerant, he flowered magically into a strapping, vibrant figure.

For the rest of the afternoon, we climbed out of the valley onto a plateau rife with long-stemmed grasses and bursting with wildflowers. The sun came out and swept everything with a golden tongue, which brought a riot of color splashing against our eyes. The smell of wood-burning fires from the nearby hills filled our nostrils with a pungent odor. One whiff was enough to make us higher than helium balloons, and we rode along at a comfortable gait, laughing and joking.

Late in the afternoon, we came upon a film crew in a valley shooting a scene from a movie. At the insistence of the newlyweds, we dismounted, set the horses out to graze, and watched. A band of outlaws had surrounded a lone kangaroo rat armed with a revolver and a knife. The kangaroo rat was played by a real kangaroo rat, a genetic mutation named Manny Effrita, a veteran of many supernatural westerns, for which the Mexican film industry is world famous. Endowed with an overabundance of energy, Manny bounded around the set, leaping over cameras and boom mikes, until the director brought him under control with the rap of a riding quirt across his buttocks. Shouting to the outlaws to pay attention, the director proceeded to pace up and down in front of the cameras describing the sort of effect he was after.

"What you must realize, *colegas*, is that we are here to capture eternity in a single incident. A group of *banditos* attacks a lone kangaroo rat for money, for gold, for cigarettes, for cocaine, what does it matter? We plot the scene, we agree on how it should be blocked out, then we rehearse, we rehearse, we rehearse until we have it down correctly. Now it is not just enough to go through the motions, to simply recreate the scene. No, we must then film it, memorialize it on a strip of celluloid. This is the key, you must understand, *compañeros!* This is what distinguishes us from the original *banditos*, who may or may not have performed this dastardly act on a kangaroo rat some fifty years ago! We are recreating it; we are taking the raw materials of history and molding them into a specific event. Not only do we have the knowledge of the historical event, but we have the power to recreate it. *Caramba!* Think of it! We have the power to be both the performer and spectator. Huh? No? We have the event, we know the event, we analyze it and break it into component sequences. Then we put them back together in any fashion we want, A B C D E F G H or F A E C B G D to suit our tastes. And not only that, but as we create the scene we can populate it with our own characters, ourselves even, if we choose. *Fantástico!* Where else, I ask you, can you find such spendid power, except with God Himself?"

We applauded, and the director, whose name was Jorge, bowed modestly. Effrita turned cartwheels up one

96

hill and down another, while the outlaws banged away with their revolvers. To let us savor a taste of the same power, Jorge permitted the girl to direct a take, then the boy. They were ecstatic; it was like a dream come true. Ever since they were tots watching *Leave It to Beaver* back in Ventura, they had dreamed of someday becoming a part of the film world. Now, by a stroke of rare fortune, they were directing a scene from a real movie!

The girl's voice trembled as she instructed the cast, and between each whispered direction, she rushed over and hugged the boy, who nuzzled and stroked her blond hair. The sequence went off well, and afterwards she collapsed in a fit of nervous giggling. For his part, the boy was more assertive. With the girl clutching his arm, he placed a filter on the lens to mute the throbbing afternoon colors and filmed the outlaws raking Manny Effrita's kinky hair with combs and brushes, while the rat tickled their armpits with the tip of his wiry tail.

"Only in the country do I permit such liberties," Jorge said with a beneficent grin.

Then Lacaud directed a sequence where the kangaroo rat, on the bum, is befriended by two Wobblies who share their last ration of beans with him. Overcome by their generosity, the rat does a triple somersault over an elephant tree and croons a protest lyric from the IWW songbook accompanied by the Wobblies on a cactus harp and a vibraphone constructed from the shinbones of a poisoned antelope.

We all clapped loudly. When it came my turn, I declined the baton. It had been a lot of fun, but it was late and we were getting hungry.

4.

It was almost dark when we entered the arroyo. We clattered several hundred yards along loose stones, when the walls fell back, the trough deepened, and we found ourselves in a steep canyon harboring a splendid oasis. A tiny village spread out from the banks of a blue-green lagoon, centering around a tiny square containing the remains of an old Spanish mission. Indian laurels shadowed the square, under which we took weary refuge. The *vaqueros* saw to the horses, leading them to the lagoon for a long drink and a vigorous rubdown. The rest of us prepared supper. Lacaud was an experienced cook, and under his direction we rolled and stuffed meat burritos. A case of warm Tecate beer, purchased at the local *abarrote*, helped grease the passage of sticky tortilla and chewy beef. An hour later, Jorge and his crew arrived, thirsty and famished, so we cooked up more burritos. Manny Effrita scoffed at our need for liquids but greedily gobbled two sacks of chia seeds, the ancient energy food. The effect on his already charged nervous system was astounding. Off he went around the village, bounding over wattle and daub houses with a single leap, clacking his teeth and chittering insanely. "A remarkable creature," Jorge declared, settling down with a burrito in each fist. "Temperamental, but a truly great artist."

After dinner everyone fired up, and soon the pretty little plaza was filled with clouds of cigar and cigarette smoke. The villagers backed off to avoid contaminating their lungs. The honeymooners discussed their favorite movies with Jorge. In the flickering light, their bodies were transparent, and I could see their bones and internal organs thumping faintly under the diaphanous veil of their clothing. Beneath the fabric of her $30 jeans, the girl's crotch sparkled like aluminum foil. Inside, there was no tweeter, tough and gritty, waiting to be plucked and used to fend off an invading army. All her parts were subject to dissolution when exposed to the proper heat.

Meanwhile, Lacaud stretched out against the saddle and told me about his life. He was in his early fifties, born in Bisbee, Arizona, son of a prospector and an Irish lady who ran a boarding house. His father had hunted gold for many years in the Sierra Madre mountains of Mexico. After the age of three, Robert, Jr. never saw him again. Word was that his father had discovered a fabulous lode deep in the mountains, a week's journey by mule from Durango, an old Indian mine, which the Indians had kept secret for centuries. No gold was ever seen, and neither was Lacaud, Sr., so perhaps the tale was apocryphal. However, his son believed it was true, and concluded that his father had been slain by Indians anxious to keep the location a secret.

"My father could smell gold," said Robert, Jr., lighting up another cigar. "He had an uncanny ability to spot a vein right through the ground. He was scanning a stretch of rough terrain on the western slope of the Sierras, when he came across three gringos working a placer. Later, after they became less hostile to his presence, he told them he thought they had missed the mother lode. No one ever saw him again. When I was about twenty-five, I finally tracked down the story. In an Indian village high above Hermosillo, I met an old Yaqui who claimed that he and several others had met up with my father shortly after he located the main lode. They gave him a choice—either he could leave the country or die. But my father was so gold-crazy he tried to make a deal with the Indians and cut them in on half the loot. When they realized he wasn't going to change his mind, they chopped his neck with a machete and threw his body into a ravine."

The moon came up on the melodious winch of a mockingbird, bathing the spires of the old mission in a gentling light and casting milky splashes between the shadows of the laurel trees. Anza's walk through the walls of the Caborca mission came back to me, and I wondered if circumstances here in this secluded little village would ever permit such a feat. A guitar started up on the other side of the square, accompanied by a trio of boozy voices. Probably not, I sighed, grinding out the stub of my cigar. People make themselves invisible by focusing their energies outward on a revered object. The effort requires great muscle and concentration. All paraphernalia related to the material world must be jettisoned before that kind of buoyancy can be achieved. The idea is to lighten the body of its corporeal weight so the spirit may achieve transcendency. It requires divesting yourself of all earthly baggage, including language. Anza didn't speak a word for six months before the event, or six months after. Silence is the only way to achieve such blinding rapture with the unknown. The return of the word after such prolonged isolation is like a clap of thunder, or the sound the universe made as it exploded into being.

Meanwhile, Jorge tried to interest the newlyweds in a quick sex take. The boy was for it, but the girl was reluctant. "What would you have us do?" she asked apprehensively.

"Whatever it is you do naturally when you are alone

together. It will give you a permanent record of how you looked and performed when you were young. It will become an imperishable archive in the memory of your lives. Years from now, when you are old and less interested, you will derive many hours of pleasure watching it."

"Hey, that's neat," said the boy.

The girl still wasn't convinced.

"Only when something is officially recorded, as on film, does it achieve certifiable historical value," Jorge declared. "Whatever you do, whether the most apocalyptic effort or the most casual gesture, has no legitimacy until it is memorialized in print. Film freezes your body for all time, for all people to observe and enjoy. It offers a reference point by which others may gauge the limits of their own self-consciousness. It will give you a yardstick for judging others anew, as well as endowing you with a more legitimate reality with which to intimidate and coerce.

"And besides..." And here he flashed a suave, cheesy grin. "... When else will you ever be asked by a director of international renown to perform in front of his cameras?"

The boy and girl stood up and began taking off their clothes.

5.

Lacaud and I were still awake after midnight, sloshing mescal and smoking cigars. "So where are you bound for?" I asked with a belch.

Boots and hat removed, stretched out on the blanket,

101

head propped up against the saddle, Lacaud had entered that tranquil, semi-narcotic state between dream and actuality, where words, unhitched from their objective references, surface like fish in a murky pond. "Toward San Felipe," he replied, the ash of his cigar brightening like the eye of a famished hawk. "I still have one last thread in my father's story to track down. It's possible he might have been killed by a guerilla named Pablo Ruiz. Ruiz operated in Sonora and northern Baja in the 1920s and 30s. Earlier, as a teenager, he fought with Pancho Villa's Army of Chihuahua during the revolution. When the Carranzistas got after him, he used to hole up for long spells in the mountains behind Guymas. There's a rumor that around 1930 he met up with an American prospector named LeCrow or LeCraw, who had recently discovered a fabulous old Indian mine. Strapped for cash, he killed the gringo and went through his packs but only found a handful of jade. Ruiz is still alive today, a very old man, living on a *rancheria* south of San Felipe on the Gulf of California. I'm going to try and find him and see if he was the man who killed my father."

"Are you saying your father may have been killed twice?"

"Something like that. My father was a man of multiple personalities. He may even have been more than one person. My mother claimed the man she married was really two people, physically identical, but different in character. At various times she lived with both. She never knew when one would leave and the other move in. Both were kind to her and claimed to love her. Though they looked alike, the feel of their bodies was different, they made love in different ways, with different outputs of energy. No one else in Bisbee ever saw

102

more than one Robert Lacaud, Sr. at a time, except my mother. One night, she was in Douglas, Arizona, sitting with my father in the lobby of the Gadsden Hotel, when the other Robert Lacaud walked up to the desk. After checking in, he walked right past where they were sitting without even nodding. The Robert Lacaud sitting with her on the sofa didn't look up or let on like he saw the man. That night, she says, she was made love to by two different men, both bearing the same face and body, but with different methods of lovemaking. And that's the night she says that I was conceived—March 2, 1925.

"So you see, I really don't know which of the two Robert Lacauds was my father, though, interestingly enough, I have a much clearer idea of who the killer of each man was. The idea of performing two separate actions to destroy what was essentially one person intrigues me. My father's dual identity wasn't simply a matter of one person being the fellow he actually was and the other the person he wanted secretly to become. Both Robert Lacauds were exactly what they wanted to be— prospectors. Both had this uncanny knack for locating gold, though neither was especially adept at mining it. My mother never complained; she claimed she got two good men for the price of one. Who knows, if, after meeting with Ruiz, I won't discover that he is very much like my father, formed in the same image, only a bandit instead of a prospector? There has been a rumor to that effect. Before she died, my mother whispered to me that there was a *third* Robert Lacaud, an outlaw and revolutionary who lived in Mexico, but who really was of gringo origin. She never saw this version or consorted with him. But if this Ruiz is really another Robert Lacaud, then my father will turn out to be his own murderer, though, at the time of the slaying, the murderer was too blinded by his own disguise to realize he was actually doing himself in! Think about that. Can a man, capable of reproducing himself by whatever process, lose touch to the degree that he mistakenly kills the parent identity from which he evolved? And which Robert Lacaud was it who fathered me, the original or the copy? And, as his son, may I not also have a double somewhere, who looks exactly like me, talks like me, walks like me, but who *feels* differently upon contact? Jorge is about my age, for instance. We resemble one another, we have the same walk, the same manner of speaking—perhaps we really are doubles. Perhaps, if you shave off his mustache and cut my hair and give us both a bath we will turn out to be the same person. It's very perplexing. I wish there were a way to unravel it."

I thought about this awhile. "What if I shoot you?"

"What would that do?"

"There's a chance that for a split-second before you die you would know for certain whether Jorge was your double or not. Sometimes death can bring that kind of insight."

"That's too big a chance to take," he said. "What if I didn't realize anything?"

"You'd die in vain then, I guess."

"To hell with that. Shoot Jorge instead."

I laughed and gulped some mescal.

"Recognizing multiple identities is more exciting than discovering gold," declared Lacaud, Jr. "Now, at last, we have proof that reality exists in multiple layers, some different, some mere duplicates of others, but all linked together by the same keys and signatures. Acknowledging and interpreting those keys and signatures be-

104

comes the great lifework of an individual. Consciousness of oneself, then, becomes a matter of vertical ascension through these layers, one layer building out of the other, to the point where one comes to realize that these different but kindred layers are all there is, and it is possible to coexist in all of them simultaneously with the same dedication and intensity."

6.

Before dawn Jorge woke us up. "Come," he whispered, "a terrible thing has happened."

In the middle of the plaza the newlyweds were locked in a frigid embrace, the girl impaled on the horn of the boy, bent over, her nipples brushing his stiff mouth. Beneath her icy gaze lurked a stricken expression like that of an animal trapped under the surface of a frozen lake. Lacaud and I obtained a quick look before the villagers threw a blanket over them.

Jorge was distraught. "I don't know what happened," he said. "We were filming and everything was going fine. They were approaching orgasm, and we were shooting them from two different angles, front and back, when *both* cameras ran out of film at the same time. The *same* instant! Ah! Ah! Never has that happened to me before in a long and distinguished career of film making! The result, gentlemen, is as you see now. The camera stopped, and they stopped too. *Muerto.* We tried to revive them, but nothing. What luck . . . what stupendous bad luck!"

CHAPTER VI

1.

On the afternoon of the following day, a Thursday, we arrived in Ensenada. It was a splendid day, the sky fleeced with stringy clouds, a bright sun boiling overhead, and a strong wind barreling in off the Pacific to bathe our faces with salty kisses. We came over a final chain of hills north and east of the city and reined in to view the panorama. Located along the upper crescent of Todos Santos Bay, the city fanned out from a level basin across a series of undulating ridges before dribbling out in empty lots and deadend streets at the foot of the mountains. A snug harbor, protected from the ocean by a rocky sea wall, sheltered a trio of merchant steamers, plus scores of fishing boats. At the north end of the city stood the dead crater of the volcano known as La Vigla. Along the waterfront were three- and four-story buildings, a jumble of architectural designs splashed with gaudy colors. At the south end of town stood a gloomy *pescadero*, its towering, soot-blackened stacks belching out greasy fumes of processed tuna and albacore.

The sight threw Manny Effrita into a dither, and he bounced and capered over the hills, turning cartwheels and leaping thirty feet into the air. The city was not for him, so he hovered on the outskirts, hurling jibes and insults and waiting for the call from Jorge to do another scene. The tainted air from the bubbling *pescadero* aggravated his sensitive kidneys, and he stayed well upwind from the offender, studying his lines and performing fantastic acrobatic tricks that kept the country people rocking with laughter.

The rest of the film crew melted into the city to become waiters and busboys and street cleaners. Jorge had run out of both money and film and needed to have a long talk with his creditors. His outlaw saga was half-completed, but the great director was in no hurry to finish it. He intended to sample the fleshpots, take in a little fishing, and visit his favorite vegetarian restaurants. Once he obtained the money, he would cruise through town on a Vespa, piping a prearranged signal on a bosun's whistle, and the crew would assemble in an abandoned school yard. Manny Effrita would bound down from the mountains, the remainder of the script would be hammered out, and they would take off for the hills to complete their epic.

To the *vaqueros*, Enseñada was a blistering metropolis, a pot to jump into and boil away the grime of the bush. She beckoned like a mermaid on a rocky shoal. They licked the dust off their lips and tugged at their knotted crotches. "Well, *señor*," said one, "this is the place you wanted to see. I hope you find what you are looking for."

"*Gracias, amigo.* I hope so too." With my tongue I touched the staple clamped to the inside of my mouth. Sunday night, whether I was ready or not, it had to come out, and I would change back into a rubbery green maverick. I had but three days left to locate the message in Hidalgo's beard.

At the bottom of the hill, I gave up my horse. Then I shook hands with the cowboys and started on foot into town. Hetty had said the bust was in a little park off the Avenida Primera near the waterfront, so I headed in that direction, full of hope and good cheer. A town of 60,000, located on the curve of a spendid bay, rife with history and tradition, had much to celebrate. My apprehensions increased as I passed square after square filled with tributes in bronze and marble to great heroes like Emiliano Zapata, Pancho Villa, Felipe Angeles, Lorenzo Cardenas, and Father Salvatierra; but none to Hidalgo. I took a deep breath and kept moving.

I had another clue: the *vaqueros* claimed to have seen the bust at one time or another, when they were both drunk and sober. "It is elusive, *señor*," they said. "First you will see it one place, then another. It never stands still. It is always moving."

"But it is a bust, isn't it? The face of Miguel Hidalgo?"

"Oh yes! But this face is... how do you say?... very *móvil*. It does not like to stay in one place a long time. It likes to move from place to place *muy rapido*.

With long, loping strides I proceeded along the elevated sidewalks under a thickening mantle of clouds. Tram wires hummed overhead like a tree full of cicadas. Gathering speed, I turned off the Avenida Machero onto the Calle Miramar. It felt good to stretch my legs after two days in the saddle, and feel the soft crust of the asphalt under my heels. Every so often I passed a smashed car, flattened by some awesome force. Glass littered the street, along with scraps of metal and a few squashed dogs. When I asked an old man what the mess was, he shrugged and pointed at the sky.

"Rain?" I said. "High winds?"

"*Quien sabe?*" he mumbled. His face was a mass of wrinkles, but with a swipe of his hand his cheeks smoothed out till they resembled a young boy's. A moment later they dissolved into a puddle of cracks and fissures.

"Can you show me the way to the Avenida Primera?" I shouted. "I need to locate the bust of Miguel Hidalgo!"

His eyes widened and a toothless grin tore open his ravaged mouth. Creaking over, he pinched my knee with his thorny fingers and pointed to my feet. "Have you speedy shoes, *señor?*" he chortled. "Are your feet quick enough to dance in all directions at once?"

I frowned in bewilderment. He chuckled again and slapped my shoulder. "Keep going," he instructed, jabbing his finger to the west and grinning broadly: "Keep going . . . keep going." His hand, gnarled and bony, but with sparkling knuckles, reached out and gave me a gentle shove.

Stoking my legs into high gear, I shot past a line of grubby pawn shops and curio stalls, clutching my duffel under my arm. A rodeo ring loomed to the left, shrouded in dust kicked up by a band of *charros* practicing lariat tricks. Calle Miramar dipped down a gentle incline to a crowded intersection strung with wires and an ornately scrolled traffic light. Without pause, I wove between a mass of bumpers and started up a slope past several cantinas reeking of smoke and tequila. Reaching Avenida Primera, I turned south, guided by blind instinct, my heart thumping wildly. Past a row of leatherwork shops I raced; the pungent, sweaty odor of saddles and harnesses gripped my nostrils and fairly lifted me off my feet and over the head of a shoeshine boy toweling the boots of a fat man with a withered arm that drooled down his right side like a worm.

Two blocks from the harbor a heavy rumbling shook

the ground. Thinking it was an earthquake, I darted out into the street only to be sternly directed to the curb by a policeman. The rumbling continued, swaying the wires spanning the street and disturbing a flock of pigeons, which began cooing in dismay. There was no panic in the faces of the other pedestrians—like veterans of a bomb-scarred city, they threw themselves into doorways or flattened their bodies against the walls.

A half-block away, a gigantic gold object flashed into view, then disappeared. Across the street I dashed, hurdling a fire hydrant and speeding down a hill toward the harbor. A moment later I came out onto an empty boulevard lined with puny, leafless trees. Across from me was a park, fringed with pallid shrubs and peeling green benches. A trio of flat, empty pedestals, each one wide enough to park a car on, took up most of the space. A soldier with a machine gun stood in front, peering nervously around. The rumbling intensified, and his face went white with fear. Working the action, he triggered a burst into the air that startled a pack of gulls. Amid a shower of birdshit I sank to the pavement and spun the wheel of a mangled bicycle—the remains of its rider lying not too far off, crushed by some inexplicable force.

2.

"So you saw the head, eh?" the man was saying.

"Yes . . . a glimpse . . . that's all."

"Stick around. You'll see it again." He signaled the bartender for another tequila sour. "And bring one for my friend!"

Before he left for San Felipe, Lacaud told me that if I

111

wanted to find out anything about Enseñada to go to Hussong's, a popular cantina on Calle Miramar. I went there, and after an hour of brooding and drinking alone struck up a conversation with a Mr. Malcolm Edward Dreeves, of Pueblo, Colorado, late retired executive of the J. C. Penney Company. An energetic man in his late sixties, with a long face pitted with tiny chuckholes, Dreeves wore his hair in a squared-off flattop, the hairs stiffened with copious applications of petroleum jelly. His nose was straight, his eyes green and scintillant. He smoked Viceroys, one right after the other, lining up the charred filters in a tight circle around his loose change and lighter.

"You stay here a day or two and you can't miss them," he declared.

"*Them?* You mean there's more than one?"

"By my count there are three. Three shiny, golden heads that have the run of this town. Before 1967, they were permanently installed on pedestals in the little park you saw by the harbor. Late that year, November I believe it was, a quake hit the city and rolled them off. They been rolling ever since, through the streets and down the avenues and along the boulevards. When the *matones* from the coast tried to take the town back in 1971, the heads played a vital role in hurling them back. That's why their cavorting is tolerated, even though they've caused a lot of grief and damage here in the city. To most folks they're heroes, the great Mexican heroes reincarnated."

"Is Hidalgo one of them?"

"Yep. And the other two are Juarez and Carranza."

Three of them, for Christ's sakes! I finished my drink and ordered another.

112

"Their behavior is greatly influenced by the moon. Whenever it gets full, they get frisky. It's almost full now, or will be in a day or so."

The tables behind the bar were filling up with local sports dressed in slacks and crisp white shirts, and tourists from California in sandals and gaudy T-shirts.

"Hidalgo is the one I'm interested in."

"He's around, he's around," said Dreeves, snorting a fresh Viceroy. "I saw him last night on the Boulevard Costera, rolling like a cannonball straight from the mouth of Hell."

"Well, I better start looking for him."

"Don't waste your energy, bub. He'll come rolling down Miramar in a little while. Full moon is when they're most active. They roll around town all month, but during the full moon they really get up a head of steam."

"But isn't that dangerous? I saw a guy on a bicycle this afternoon who looked like he'd been mashed by a bulldozer."

"You bet. But these heads are regarded as heroes in Ensenada. See, in '71, the *matones* up the coast made a bid to take the city. They had tanks, machine guns, rocket launchers, everything. I wasn't here then, but I heard all about it when I arrived in '74. The *matones* launched a two-pronged assault right down Highway One and around the east flank of La Vigla mountain. The townsfolk were organized into militia cadres, and they fought well, but, hell, the *matones* were CIA-trained and armed with the latest hardware. They drove down the highway past the harbor, practically to the Plaza Reforma, just a few blocks from here. Meanwhile, the other column slipped down the road around the east slope of La Vigla and forced the defenders there to fall clear back

113

into the city, almost here to Calle Miramar."

He paused to signal the barkeep for a tequila sour and fired up another Viceroy.

"What happened then?"

"Well, it was full-moon time, toward the middle of the month, and them heads had been rolling around town since sun-up, over in the eastern section and out south, perky as colts with a hardon. But when the *matones* come over the mountain there and threatened to link up with the other column pushing in from the docks, well, all hell broke loose. Whether the earth tilted abruptly, or a sunspot flared up, or there was another quake, nobody rightly knows. But them heads come charging up through town and hit the *matones* from three different directions. They came so fast and furious the *matones* never had a chance to train their rockets on them. Panic set in, and that band of hard-bitten cutthroats melted away like cheese under a broiler. Ever since then, them heads can do just as they damn please around this town."

A mariachi band crowded through the door and headed for the center of the floor. Next to a brick fireplace opposite the bar, the players formed a semicircle and took up their instruments. Dark-skinned men with flamboyant mustaches and pearly teeth, they played with brassy fervor, fueled by shots of brandy and mescal. After the first number, they were deluged with pesos and dollar bills that rose in glittering heaps around their ankles. The finest mariachi band in Baja Norte, "Los Potentes Lagartos," as they were known, their fiery music had rallied the citizens of Enseñada during the late crisis. It was their courageous presence that fateful day in September 1971 that some feel inspired the three golden

114

heads to give up their frollicking and come storming to the rescue. As the invading columns of *matones* battled their way into town, threatening to converge, the Lagartos marched into the Plaza Reforma through a hail of bullets playing a popular tune to bolster the sagging morale of the defenders. Whether the sound of their trumpets and guitars reached the bronze ears of the three busts is hard to say, but a few minutes later the pavement shook with a roar as the busts charged into action, scattering *matones* like quail.

The plank floor of the cantina was strewn with sawdust. Countless charcoal drawings of patrons and local celebrities papered the stucco wall over the brick fireplace. On a shelf ten feet above the floor sat a stuffed turkey vulture, its black wings swept out, scabby head cocked and leering down on the hubbub. Over the bar hung a series of sepia-tinted photographs of Enseñada around the turn of the century, including one of a sea serpent, long as an anaconda, washed up on the shores of Todos Santos Bay. Behind the bar, a team of four men hustled along a platform of wooden duckboards, opening beers and mixing drinks. A pair of waiters worked the floor, slipping between packed tables, holding trays full of *cerveza* and José Cuervo tequila. Ocherous smoke rolled along the ceiling, obscuring the ornate molding. At the back of the room a party of locals played horse dice, shouting and slapping the table with every roll. The gringos clustered around the bar and fireplace, stomping and whistling to the blasting beat of the Lagartos.

Around 10:30 a low rumbling shook the walls of the old cantina. Nobody paid much attention; the band was gone, and the crowd had thinned out. The rumbling intensified, rattling bottles behind the bar. The bartenders glanced at the door, the waiters stopped dead in their tracks, the dice players suspended their cups in mid-air, and at once everyone in the place grew quiet. The rumbling grew louder, shaking the photos on the wall, kicking dust off the plank boards. The buzzard wobbled around the shelf like it wanted to take off. Screams came from outside, cries of panic and terror, accompanied by a grinding, crunching roar. Through the door I saw people running down the street, eyes bulging, mouths agape. A moment later, a huge yellow orb rushed by with a sound like a hundred cannon going off in an abandoned quarry. There was a wild scene at the door as the patrons struggled to get out. Dreeves and I were first, and as we staggered onto the sidewalk we saw the head bumping down Calle Miramar toward the intersection.

I hitched a ride with a kid on the back of a Honda and hung on grimly as he snarled in and out of the confusion in the wake of the rampaging head. Careening from curb to curb, the orb flattened telephone poles and fire hydrants, mail boxes and newspaper kiosks. In front of the Hotel Bahia we witnessed an incredible event. A half-dozen naval cadets—dressed in greatcoats, polished shoes, and white gloves—deployed in a straight line and, with swords drawn, charged the onrushing sphere. The collision was brief but spectacular. The cadets were smashed to a pulp and their bodies smeared across the street. With a deafening roar, the head rocked around the corner and out of sight.

The Honda skidded to a halt, and I leaped off. People crept cautiously out of doorways and alleys and shook their heads at the youngsters' brash heroics. A sanitation crew, led by a quartet of weeping mothers, arrived a few

116

minutes later and began scraping up the mess.

3.

Back at Hussongs, a furious argument was in progress.
"It was Carranza!" shouted one man.
"Hidalgo!" said another.
"You're both wrong!" declared a third. "It was Juarez!"
"No!"
"Yes!"
"It was too!"
"It was not!"
"You're crazy!"
"You are babbling like a madman!"
"Juarez!"
"Hidalgo!"
"Carranza!"
"I saw it with my own eyes!"
"You have the eyes of a bat!"
"And you have the manners of a goat! Apologize!"
"I would kiss the asshole of the scurviest *puta* in Enseñada before I would ever stoop to such a thing.!"
"This is a very grave offense you have given me!"
"Hidalgo!"
"Carranza!"
"Juarez!"
"SI-LEN-CI-O! ! !"
The voice splintered the air like a crack of thunder. Tottering along the bar, banging into empty stools, leather sandals squeaking under his massive weight, came old Hussong himself, a fat, wrinkled, yellow man

117

with slit eyes, bulbous lips, and cheeks like porcelain plates that have been shattered and glued carefully back together. The stillness that came over the place was eerie. People stared at the old man in fear and awe. Estimates of his age ran as high as 90 and 95. An immigrant from Canton, he had spent his early years learning the art of the *curandero* from the Yaquis and other herb dealers of the Sierra Madre. For years he practised his trade in Durango and Chihuahua City, until the night of the great Chinese pogrom in September 1916, led by Pancho Villa. With hundreds of others, Hussong and his family fled west into Sonora and Baja, settling first in Hermosillo, then Enseñada. His powers were so strong, it was said he could make himself invisible when he wanted. It was also rumored that during the assault by the *matones* that it was Hussong who had signaled the heads to attack and drive them back. Now with both hands—soft, pudgy fingers like plugs of taffy—he swept the crowd silent, restoring calm and order. Then, with everything at a whisper, he pivoted on one heel and waddled toward the back of the room. The crowd parted obediently to let him through. At the end of the bar, he paused to survey the group through slits that looked like gun portals in a pillbox; then he disappeared.

"Every night the same argument," Dreeves growled as he turned back to his drink."

"Three heads," I whispered. *"Three* heads!"

"Yo. You don't expect the Mexicans to make it simple, do you?"

"But I thought—"

"Hey, bub, you don't *think* in this town," Dreeves cautioned. "Nobody *thinks* here. *Thinking* doesn't do any good in a place like Enseñada. You just observe and get

118

out of the way when you're supposed to. *Thinking* like you and me is used to can't begin to penetrate the confusion that envelops everything down here. You notice that Aristotle ain't one of them heads rolling around out there? Least that's what my wife tells me, and she reads all the time. Stuff goes down here you wouldn't believe. Up in the States, the mayor would've declared the place a disaster area a long time ago and called in the National Guard. But this is Mexico, owned and operated by Mexicans, and their minds don't work like ours!"

"But those other heads! What about them!"

"See, in 1960, the Mexican government erected the busts to commemorate the 150th year of Mexico's first attempt to gain independence from Spain. Three busts of three of her greatest heroes—Juarez, Carranza, and Hidalgo, the priest who started it all. When they were formally dedicated here in May of 1960, it was quite a bash. All the Baja and Sonora bigwigs came; President Lopez Mateos sent a personal envoy; Pat Brown, then governor of California, came down; Ike sent a representative from the White House. Big doings, big doings. If I hadn't been raking in all that dough for J.C. Penney up in Pueblo, Colorado, why, I would've been here too. The busts were twelve feet high and were molded out of iron at a foundry in Guadalajara. A liquid varnish made of real gold was painted on afterward. Course most of that's been chipped away from all that rolling through the streets. But you can bet when they first came off the line down there they musta sparkled like nuggets. After they were finished, the busts were transported up here by boat and placed on the pedestals you saw in that little park this afternoon. The earthquake of 1967 shook them loose and they been gallivanting around ever since."

"If they're so dangerous, how come the military hasn't blown them up?"

"Bad luck. Superstition. Plus, the people would be infuriated. Sure, the heads cause a lot of grief, but they also hurled back the *matones* at a critical time. And the *matones* could attack again, any time. The heads may be a nuisance to me and you, but to the folks of Enseñada they're sacred objects."

I took a big slug of tequila. "In one of them—Hidalgo, I was told—is a message that will enable me to unlock the mystery of all tongues and converse with the stars."

"No doubt. Well, next time he rolls down Calle Miramar, get yourself a catcher's mitt and bag the fucker."

"I'm not kidding." And I told him the story.

Dreeves looked at me calmly like he'd heard the story before, at the same bar, while sitting on the same stool. "Well, bub, as I see it, you got but one chance to find that message. Fortunately, you come to town at the right time. At twelve o'clock sharp on the night of a full moon, all three heads converge on the park and remount their pedestals. But only for ten minutes. During that ten minutes, everything in the city comes to a complete halt, and the entire population crowds into the area to pay homage. The people only stay a few minutes to pray and give thanks, then they scatter, cause as soon as the ten minutes is over them heads start wobbling, and they's off again for another month of running around the city."

"When is full moon?"

"You're in luck, bub. It's Sunday night."

"Sounds like my only chance."

"I wouldn't miss it if I was you," he said, ordering us both another drink.

120

4.

My room was in the Hotel Delibes on the Avenida Primera. A four-story, whitewashed structure named after the French composer, with a snug lobby draped with ferns and broad-leafed plants. Daguerreotypes hung from the walls, along with posters and handbills announcing the premieres of such works as *Sylvia* and *Jean de Nivelle*. The proprietor—the fat man with the withered arm I had seen earlier—believed Delibes to be the most underrated composer of the 19th century. His hotel—crammed with memorabilia, including a life-sized effigy in the lobby—was his attempt to restore that reputation to its rightful pinnacle.

Before going upstairs, I paused to select a cigar from the glass counter next to the registration desk. Underwater, in the pool, I never felt the urge to smoke. But here in Mexico, with my lungs back to normal, I got an itch to inhale something riper than automobile exhaust and the stench from the fish factory. As I leaned over, a curious sound, low and pulsating, filled my ears; an aria from *Lakmé* throbbed on the turntable behind the desk—sultry, tropical music, strangely out of place in this chilly coastal town—but the humming could not be identified with that.

I finally chose a smoke and paid the proprietor. A creole from Martinique, brought up in Puerto Rico, and a citizen of Baja California, he was conversant in many languages, including Guarani and Caddoan. His bad arm, cloaked in seersucker, drooped to his rotund waist. Three fingers, pink and lifeless as uncooked wieners, poked out the sleeve. He was fatter than Bilkstrode, a hulking dune of a figure, with round shoulders and a

121

stomach that ladled down from his throat to the precipice of a metal belt buckle. A round, malarial face stared out from under a mantle of unruly hair like a creature seen through the foliage of a canvas by Henri Rousseau.

"What is that humming?" I asked.

He nodded toward the lobby. Sitting in a chair next to the wax dummy of Delibes was a woman with dour Indian features, drooping eyes, and thick black hair. She stared at me; I stared back.

"She has been waiting for you..."

The low humming seeped through the air, crowding out the passionate strains of *Lakmé*. I looked again. The woman pulled a scarf away from her neck, revealing a deep cleavage.

"Why does she whistle like that?"

"She is *loco*. A *revolucionaria*. She thinks someday she will lead Mexico out of the wilderness and into a new Garden of Eden." He spat toward the floor, but the gob failed to clear the horizon of his belly and oozed down the front of his Acrylan shirt. "She is a *cortesana*, though she hates men."

The humming intensified, coloring the air and obscuring the pale, sensitive face of Léo Delibes standing in waxen splendor beside the seated woman. She stared at me intently through dark, luminous eyes, her lips clamped together.

"Where's the sound coming from?"

"Her. She makes it. All day. All night. It is everywhere. It drowns out my music. It drives me crazy. Someday, I will kill her."

"It's not coming from the statue?"

"No, no... I wish it were! It's coming... it comes from *la cosita*."

122

"What's that?"

"A woman's secret place."

The hair bristled on the back of my neck. My fingers poked through my pockets and latched onto the abalone mouthpiece given me by the Witiki squaw.

"She will go upstairs with you, if you wish," he said, with a look of disgust.

"No... no... I'm too tired for that."

"She doesn't charge much, and she is very professional."

"Not tonight..."

As I crossed the lobby to the elevator, the humming intensified to a throbbing pitch. The woman nodded to me and placed her right hand over her breast. I bowed formally and disappeared through the door.

5.

Hussong served a tasty breakfast, which I sat down to next morning: *Huevos rancheros*, refried beans, and hominy, overlaid with strips of green chile. I was on my second plateful, sitting at a table in the back, when Jorge Amoza, the famous movie director, came through the door. "How are you, *compañero?*" he greeted, plopping into a chair. Short, heavy-set, with smooth caramel skin, he had the classic Mayan face: sloping forehead, aquiline nose, sensuous mouth, and almond-shaped eyes, at once seductive and hypnotic, capable of making virtuous people shed their principles and perform scenarios of his own devising.

"Join me?" I said with a grin that revealed bits of egg and bean sticking to my teeth.

123

"Not that stuff," he shuddered. "I just had a *liquado:* oats, guava, raw milk, cucumber slices, yucca stalks, all threshed into a nutritious pap."

It was my turn to shudder.

"Very sad about the young people, no?"

"Did you get some good footage?"

"Excellent. They were very pretty people. Nice movements. Enough for, say, a fifteen-minute teaser. It could be shown before *Deep Throat.* A warm-up, as you gringos say."

"You don't miss a trick, do you?"

"Nothing is wasted. That is my motto. Film it now, I always say. You can cut it later, but if it's not in print you won't have the choice."

"Let me buy you a drink."

"A little early," said Jorge, consulting a digital watch. "But, since you are buying, perhaps just one little campari and soda. With a twist."

I signaled the waiter.

"And you, my gallant *norteamericano* friend, how are you coming with your quest?" Jorge asked, after toasting me with his glass.

"Not very well. Last night I found out there are three busts, of which Hidalgo is one. All three have the run of the town. They go anywhere they want, smashing and pulverizing. The period of full moon is the worst; they are always on the move. Sunday night they will return to their pedestals for about ten minutes. I'll have to make my bid then."

"I am very interested in your quest," said Jorge. "It is very biblical, this search for the Word, the key that will unlock the secret of all tongues. All my films are concerned with this theme. Twenty years ago I did a film

124

with Gilbert Roland about this very subject. It was called *Tongue-Zot*, and was about a man whose tongue had been tied in knots at infancy by his cruel stepfather. He wanders around Oaxaca looking for something or someone to untie his tongue so he can speak. Maybe you saw the film? It was shown at festivals at Bordeaux, at Orvieto, at Zagreb, at Bogata, at Tampa, at Helsinki. Ingmar Bergman said it influenced the whole course of his work. Not bad, eh? Well, the hupshot... hipshot?... is that Roland unravels his tongue enough to speak Mixtec with the Indians, but not Spanish. A knotted tongue being associated with arcane languages, you see. He speaks to a few people, but not many, not many. But who knows what wonderful things he relates? No one, because I could not find anyone to translate the Mixtec for me. Even the people who spoke it in Oaxaca wanted to keep it a secret. There is a rather spicy scene... it was deleted for *norteamericano* audiences... where Roland goes down on an old Indian woman... but that only knots his tongue tighter, and he disappears into a ravine to join a pack of javalinas who, miraculously, understand every word he says. In Colombia, critics hailed the film as a passionate diatribe against the unnatural pleasure of cunnilingus; but I think they missed the point. The film is about something altogether different. I wrote the script myself. Ah, if the world only knew... writers invent reality, which filmmakers then popularize, which people then live. A complex film, very, very... but literary, literary... like so many of my films."

Old Hussong waddled by with an imperceptible nod—massive, stately, rattling the floorboards with his ponderous weight.

"Someday... someday... I would like to do a film

125

about that man," Jorge sighed, tracking the Chinaman's backside through a viewfinder looped around his neck. "If only Sydney Greenstreet were still alive."

"What about Orson Welles?"

"After paying his salary, I couldn't afford a roll of film. Besides, I don't think he understands what power is about. Hussong is willing to make himself invisible, which is why he is a man of true power. Welles would never take that chance."

I devoured the rest of my breakfast and sat back and lit up a cigar.

"It may be of interest to you to come with me today," said Jorge.

"Why?"

"I have been asked by the Mexican government to do an aerial survey of Enseñada showing the paths taken by the three heads as they roll through the streets. The government is interested in finding out if they follow any pattern, and if perhaps the force that animates them can be ascertained, and maybe... maybe...harnessed for export to help redress our lamentable balance of payments."

"I have only two days," I said. "Sunday night will be my only chance to check Hidalgo's beard for the message. That's cutting it awfully close. What if I get hit by a car or come down with the flu before I can get near him?"

"What if there are hundreds of star-struck gringos just like you here in the city waiting for the same moment to search for the same message?" Jorge said, rattling the ice cubes in his empty glass.

My stomach churned violently.

At the tiny airport south of town, Jorge introduced me to his cinematographer, a man of European origin named

Bally Blitzen. "Hah low," Bally said tonelessly, giving my hand a squeeze. His body looked like it was stuffed with old newspapers. A round man with a round face and a round neck that bulged over his collar. A brown man with brown eyes, brownish skin, and brown lips. Wearing a chauffeur's cap, high-button shoes, knickers, and a bow tie.

A military helicopter, rigged with an Arriflex camera, had been placed at our disposal. We squeezed in—Jorge, Bally, myself, and the pilot—and took off about noon. For two hours we cruised over the city recording the erratic path of the busts. It was a fair day, the sun glimmering through a film of haze. Smoke from dozens of fires curled up sluggishly to thicken the air. At the south end of town, near the airport, the twin stacks of the *pescadero*, the city's main industry, spat out a furry, licorice column.

There seemed no discernible pattern to the heads's behavior. They rolled aimlessly through the streets, cornering sharply or barreling through intersections. Dogs, bicyclists, vendors went down under the onslaught. Approaching one another, however, they veered to opposite sides and passed by unscathed. "So," Jorge shouted over the roar of the chopper, "they respect each other's presence! That must tell us something!"

But what? Other than that gesture, the energy displayed by the heads seemed random and meaningless. Like gods on Olympus or members of the United States Senate, they didn't care what they did to others, so long as they protected themselves. Ceaselessly they rolled through the streets, squashing and destroying. From the air it was obvious that the people of Enseñada had developed quick reflexes. Walking to work, waiting for a

127

schoolbus, delivering packages, strolling with friends, they were alert for any sign of the heads, like pioneers on the lookout for hostile Indians.

Jorge looked up from his binoculars. "This is craziness!" he shouted. "I see no pattern down there! But then maybe the camera will pick something up. There's no geometric sequence to what they do. They don't move around in squares, rectangles, or circles. There's no hesitation or self-consciousness either. They come to an intersection and shoot right through! Or turn, bam! like that."

"Dey korner werry smootly," Bally observed, his eye glued to the lens of the Arriflex.

"They don't go up in the mountains, they don't go on the highway, they don't smash through houses or cut through alleys, they stay strictly in the streets, they rarely jump on the sidewalks!" I yelled. Yet it was obvious, from the power they had, that the heads could go anywhere—down the peninsula to La Paz, across the Pacific to China, around the world to Moscow.

After two hours, I got the impression that I was observing a force every bit as mammoth and inexhaustible as the natural flow of the tides or the wind. Only this force had no purpose except to maim and destroy, intimidate and disrupt. "Smash," "squash," "flatten," and "crunch" were mere descriptive labels applied by us to a power that could neither be avoided nor understood. It was simply there, an ineluctable thrust in the convulsion of life, and no amount of pleading or supplicating could influence or mitigate its force. The heads were alive in all their implacable fury, and to survive them a person had to develop instincts for detection and withdrawal rivaling those of a pigmy in a rain forest.

My hopes for locating the message in Hidalgo's beard sank rapidly. All that rolling around for the last ten years had most likely jarred it loose. The message might be anywhere, on any street in Enseñada, a scrap of paper fluttering in a gutter.

Back at the airport, Jorge put his arm around my shoulder. "Sunday night then, *compañero*, you have an appointment with destiny, no?"

"Yeah."

"Mr. Blitzen and I would like to be there to memorialize that moment... eh, Bally?"

"Uf kurse."

"Appointments with destiny occur all too infrequently in our lives," Jorge declared. "May I draw up a contract covering the details?"

"I'll sign whatever you want," I said wearily.

6.

I didn't stir from my room for the rest of the afternoon. At 6:30, Dreeves knocked on my door. I shouted at him to go away, but he persisted, citing the recuperative powers of tequila mixed with lemon juice and flavored with maraschino cherries. At Hussong's, we mounted the bar and dove straight into a bottle of José Cuervo, without benefit of fins or snorkel. By 9:00, we were mired at the bottom, wrestling with the pickled worm, Dreeves belching Viceroy smoke in the worm's face, me babbling insanely. By 10:00, I was back in my room, vomiting into the sink. The walk home was like a strip of celluloid that someone had partially erased with his finger. The heads were frolicking through the streets like frat brothers on a

129

Saturday night. Miraculously, through no effort of my own, I avoided getting smashed: a shoeshine boy tripped me up before I could hurl myself into the path of an onrushing sphere; a young blade and his *novia* shoved me into a doorway just as I was about to dive off the curb. Back in the stifling hold of my room in the Hotel Delibes, I got the dry heaves and lay on the bed writhing in convulsions till my stomach finally smoothed out, and I slipped into a deep, swampy sleep.

In this dream I was in a bookstore asking the proprietor for a copy of the latest biography of the well-known chameleon and pulcinello, Navvy Dypes. He pulled the volume out of a waste can and I stared at the genealogical charts inside and the old photographs of my friends and family, but there were none of me, not even a Polaroid snapshot. There were lithographs of my home town in Missouri, a biographical sketch of Colonel Alexander Doniphan, and maps of the street where I grew up and the schools I attended, marked with X's and connected by dashes to indicate the routes I had used getting from one place to another.

It was just getting light—Sunday morning—when the door creaked open and a woman whisked silently across the tiled floor in rubber-soled sandals. Music waffling in behind her, the overture to *Coppélia*, woke me up, and when I opened my eyes she was sitting on the edge of the bed staring down at me like a fish hawk at a tender salmon in a shallow pool. "Would you like something from me?" she whispered, placing her hand on my crotch. "It will cost you ten dollars or 200 pesos. It's late, or I'd charge you more."

"Who are you?" I said hoarsely. My throat felt like a porcupine had been stuffed down it.

"Marta. I work the floor of this hotel." She squeezed my testicles, but nothing happened. My pecker lay wilted against my thigh like an anchovy in a salad bowl.

"None for me, thanks."

She stared at me, trying, in the thin light that seeped through the shuttered windows, to determine who I was.

"Navvy *Norteamericano*," I said helpfully.

"Ah... from California?"

"Yes."

She pulled her hand away and stood up. "You don't cater to *gringos*?" I said.

"Of course... but it's late... and I'm very tired."

A faint humming filled the room, soft and chirruping like a pair of doves calling to one another in a tree. "Wait," I croaked, throwing aside the covers. "Stay... just a little while... I have some beer ... some Balkan ovals...."

I opened two warm Carta Blancas and handed her one. "It's a bit late, isn't it, Marta, to be plying your trade?"

Her face was old and heavy, her cheeks sagged in flaccid rolls to her jaw. But her mouth was taut and her eyes seethed with a smoldering fury. I was surprised to discover she was exactly my age.

"It's the best time," she replied. "Very late at night a man gets desperate for sleep and will pay anything for a pill to knock himself out."

"Tequila did it for me last night," I sighed.

"I thought you were someone else," she said.

"Oh?"

"The *matones* get very lonely up on the coast. Occasionally, they slip into town for some refreshment."

"But you couldn't possibly...?"

"Of course not. Do you think I'm a traitor? It is a way we have of curing them forever of their bad habits. I use my sex as a lure to tempt them, and when they bite I . . ."

She drew a knife out of her waistband and flashed it. The humming intensified, drowning out the strains of *Coppélia* wafting up from the lobby. I shivered and drew my feet up off the floor.

"The *matones* are pigfuckers, and every one we kill today spares us from having to kill another tomorrow."

"They must be a pretty rotten bunch."

"What they have done to the workers and peasants in their own countries is bad enough. But listen, *gringo*, five years ago they did something here in Enseñada that hardened the hearts of every living soul against them forever. You know about the attack in 1971?"

"Yes."

"This was even more treacherous . . ."

It was the fiesta of *La Posada*, which falls a few days before Christmas. The children of Enseñada, rich and poor, were invited to the *charro* downtown to watch fireworks, eat candy, and receive presents. Three enormous *piñatas*, shaped like donkeys, were wheeled into the arena. The master of ceremonies, the vice-alcalde of the city, led the children up to the papier-mâché replicas. But when the sides fell apart, twelve *matones* with machine guns leaped out and began firing. Chaos engulfed the arena as the children scattered in every direction, wailing with terror. The local militia reacted quickly—a company of shock troops surrounded the *charro*, sharpshooters climbed the walls, a helicopter buzzed overhead. Fortunately, the quick thinking of the vice-alcalde saved many lives. After herding the surviving children into a tunnel under the arena, a signal was sent—by whom nobody knows—and the heads of Hidalgo and Benito Juarez arrived a few minutes later. Luckily, it was the time of the full moon, when the heads are most active. What happened next is told with pride today in every home in Enseñada: swiftly and relentlessly, the heads tracked down each *matone* and flattened him.

"Who ... *what* ... are these heads?" I said.

"They are the incarnations of the spirit of liberty and justice that burn vibrantly in the souls of the oppressed throughout Mexico and the rest of the world," she exclaimed rapturously.

"But the heads rampage through the streets slaughtering innocent people! I've seen them with my own eyes!"

"Yes. Their power is so great it is indiscriminate at times. People think an earthquake or an atom bomb or a prayer will contain the heads and direct them back to their pedestals. This is naive. Only justice—social and economic justice for oppressed peoples everywhere—will restore the heads to their rightful places. And the only way to achieve this is through revolution—total, cleansing revolution. The *matones* and their capitalist sponsors must be scourged from the face of Mexico. They cannot be reasoned with, or pardoned, or appeased, or granted special dispensation. They must be exterminated, along with the politicos who allowed them sanctuary on our coast."

"Have you the power to make the heads stop rolling?" I said.

"Alone ... no ... I am nothing. But together ... collectively ..."

"But you can ... *appeal* to them in a special way?"

133

"As a woman . . . yes . . . as a revolutionary . . ."

"I have no influence over them. I am completely at their mercy."

"You are a *gringo* . . . what do you expect?"

"But in one of them . . . Hidalgo . . . there is a message for me."

"The heads contain many messages."

"Tomorrow night, when they settle on their pedestals, I will have only ten minutes to find it. I'm afraid that won't be long enough."

"My people have waited 450 years," she said coldly. "Surely, you can do your business in ten minutes."

"But I need more time! Ten minutes is nothing! And if I don't find the message in ten minutes I will have come all this way for nothing! I'll go back to California empty-handed! My father will put me in the hospital and Doctor Bilkstrode will tear out my gills and remold my lungs! You've got to help me, Marta! Please!"

She looked at me with icy contempt. "It's late," she muttered, sliding off the bed.

I grabbed her wrist. "Come with me tomorrow night! I'll pay you anything you want! I can't do it alone. I need you there with me!"

"Your quest, *gringo,* to unlock the mystery of tongues, does not interest me," she hissed, flattening her eyes into a hateful squint. "For me, the heads speak the hope of only one tongue: justice for my people. My energies as a woman and a revolutionary are directed solely toward that end. Go chase the spirit energy in your own country, if your country has any spirit energy left. Leave my country alone. You are nothing more than another god-damn Yankee imperialist trying to rob Mexico of what is rightfully hers! Leave us both alone and go back to your country!"

"Please . . . Marta . . . I need your help. I can't do this alone. Please help me!"

I followed her off the bed, clutching the beer bottle. The humming nagged at my ears like the wings of a pesky fly. She reached the door but before she could turn the handle I slugged her on the head. Hard enough to coldkonk her. My hands shook and a spume of sour beer churned up my throat. In her waistband was the knife— short, stubby, razor-sharp. The thought occurred to me that I was operating out of an instinct as base as any of those that had tried to thwart me in the past, but I brushed the thought aside and got down to business. Marta had something I needed. Turning her over on her back, I raised her skirt and knelt down between her thighs.

7.

I woke again around noon, feeling refreshed. Marta's clandestine visit had boosted my sagging spirits. I had now in my possession a powerful instrument that I could use, if necessary, to make the heads remain still.

There wasn't much time. In twelve hours Hetty's spell would wear off and I would be stranded in Mexico—a hulking green monster with webbed feet and a clicking voice; a prime candidate for canning in the local fish factory.

The lobby was filled with the rapturous strains of *Sylvia*. The one-armed proprietor had pushed all the furniture aside and, dressed in a sharkskin jogging outfit, was lurching through an intricate *pas de deux* with a buxom

135

woman in sequined shorts. I begged off their invitation to join in, citing acute hunger and thirst.

The streets were gray and dreary, the sky overcast with a gloomy pallor, through which the sun struggled to peep. Rosary-strung dwarfs, returning from their favorite place of worship, thronged the sidewalks. The electric wires spanning the Avenida Primera howled a mournful threnody which set my teeth on edge. Two blocks from the hotel a streetcar lay with its spine crushed amid a heap of twisted metal and shattered wood. The face of the streetcar was intact, and several beggar women were polishing the nose and empty headlights, whispering consolingly and offering sympathetic pats.

I lunched at Henry's, a little café across from the Hotel Bahia. Spanish omelette, asparagus *con chile*, and prickly pear soup, washed down with a glass of *damiana* tea. Tourists milled around the shops outside, flown in for a day's excursion from San Diego, to buy mallets and hacksaws, ice tongs and tweezers, collanders and letter openers, for which the craftsmen of Enseñada are famous.

I headed for the beach to unlimber my legs. South of town, the sand was littered with the bodies of drowned Japanese fishermen. Hungry gulls cried overhead, waiting for the corpses to ripen. Next to a stagnant breakwater, a Mexican artillery unit was lobbing shells far out into the bay, ostensibly to gain a little target practice, but in reality slaying hundreds of sea bass and corvina which later would be gathered in nets. The stench off the water was putrid, a far cry from the odors glowingly detailed in the travel brochures.

To my left, behind the beach, loomed the bleak, forbidding mountains of Baja, bare as the tonsure of a

136

novitiate priest. Out of this waste, at approximately 3:30 that afternoon, a huge black bull stumbled, spiked around the eyes and mouth with cholla thorns. Suffering fearsome torments, the bull staggered soundlessly toward the water and disappeared beneath the swelling waves, his tail stiff with anguish.

All afternoon I tramped the polluted strand, uncovering shells and turning over rocks. Under one, a chamber orchestra of hermit crabs was grinding out a creditable version of a suite by Carlos Chavez. Jellyfish splattered the sand in oozy blots. Gigantic turtles, on their way to the Enchantadas, rested warily on the beach, drawn up in a circle with their young huddled protectively inside. In mossy whispers they told me how far they had come, how long they planned to stay, and how far they had to go to reach a destination that, by all accounts, was drifting out of the range of even the strongest amongst them.

Later, I came upon the head of a man sticking up out of the sand. A bald head with a furry red mustache and round, staring eyes pointing out into the bay. When I tried to pass in front, a voice cried, "Don't! You'll cut off his vision! He is a very great poet from New England who has never observed a Pacific sunset before!" I looked around, but couldn't locate the voice. Perhaps the poet was a ventriloquist? An hour later, retracing my steps toward town, I watched a gang of boys kick the head around in a spirited soccer game. From somewhere a voice over a loudspeaker was shrieking in protest.

Jorge waved a ream of papers at me as I stumbled into Hussong's. "Sign here ... and here ... and here," he said, signaling the waiter, who brought a tray of foaming beer and Dorrito chips.

"Navvy, this little deal ... win or lose ... is going to

137

make you a bundle," Dreeves remarked through a cloud of cigarette smoke.

Jorge's cameraman, Bally Blitzen, went over me with a tape measure and ran a light meter up and down my cheeks like an electric razor.

"Let me drink in peace," I said, blowing the cream off the beer and knocking back half of it in a single gulp.

"Showtime is 11:30," Jorge announced. "You need to wear white so you'll stand out. Bally got you an outfit this afternoon." He held up a pair of *huaraches,* a linen tunic, and trousers. "We'll want your hair darker, so before you reach the park rub a little of this in." He handed me a bottle. "See to it, will you, Dreeves?"

"You can count on me, J. A."

"I'll give you last-minute instructions at the park. Mainly what I want is a frantic search, with you turning your face toward us every minute or so. Remember that, Navvy... we'll only have one camera on you, so we'll need your cooperation. When you find the message, I want a look of exultation... grins, prayers, fervent thanks, smiles... okay?"

I think I ate something; I don't remember. When Bally and Jorge finally left to set up the camera in the park, I heaved a sigh of relief. "You'll have plenty of time, Navvy, ten minutes is a long time, so take it easy and look the head over carefully," Dreeves counseled. "Don't leave any nook or cranny untouched. Look in the nostrils, look in the ears, look between the lips... everywhere. Don't panic. Even when the heads start teetering, you'll still have a couple of minutes. Trust me. I've observed this little ritual before. I'll be in front of the crowd with a clock on you, calling out the time at sixty-second intervals. The final two minutes I'll call out at fifteen-second intervals. I'll be right there with you, bub. When there's nothing left in the breadbox but a few crumbs, you can always count on Malcolm Edward Dreeves."

Soon as it got dark I went to the men's room and changed into the linen outfit and rubbed the dye into my hair. At the bar when I came out was a shot glass full of a bright amber liquid. "The old man... this is from him... with best wishes," said Dreeves in an awe-stricken voice.

The liquid tasted cool and refreshing. At the bottom of the glass Hussong's face flashed into view, ponderous and benign, before slipping away with the last drop.

The liquid settled in a warm pool in my stomach and sent vigorous tentacles surging through my veins. As we stepped outside, my head cleared and my muscles relaxed. It was only 11:00, but already the streets were crowded with people heading for the park. The moon, round and orange as a pumpkin, had cleared the mountains to the east and was beaming warmly through a string of clouds.

The park was jammed with people. Jorge and Bally had set the camera up on a bench a hundred feet from the pedestals. Spectators swarmed around, jostling the tripod. Bally cursed them vigorously and kicked out with his feet.

"I want lots of worried looks at first!" Jorge shouted in my ear. "Frantic, hand-wringing gestures... then you find it... and *when* you find it... turn back to us and smile... remember... SMILE!"

My eyes felt sharp as daggers. Hussong's potion had cranked me up to a keen pitch—my mind was alert; my body hummed like a generator.

139

By 11:30 the park was filled. Dreeves and I pushed off from the bench and elbowed our way toward the empty pedestals. Jorge swept the crowd with a powerful light, while Bally pressed the shutter and recorded our progress. In front of each pedestal stood a tight-lipped soldier with a machine gun. Dreeves and I squirmed up to the foot of the middle pedestal and waited. A few minutes later a ripple went through the crowd, and with a calm, unhurried motion, so unlike their behavior on the streets, the people fell back, opening a corridor down which the first head bumped and rumbled. At the steps leading to the mounting the head bounced up, and with another little bounce, effortless as a tennis ball, rocked onto the pedestal and grew still. Two minutes later it was joined by the others, flashing brilliantly in the moonlight, one coming straight west from Avenida Primera, the other down Boulevard Cesteros from the harbor. Again, without fanfare or panic, the crowd fell back, forming two lanes, down which the heads rolled to their respective niches.

At two minutes before midnight, all three heads were settled firmly in place. Due to the movement of the crowd, I didn't get a clear look at them as they passed through to their mountings. Caught in a backwash of spectators closing the lanes, Dreeves and I found ourselves on the left of the line paralleling the pedestals. "Now!" Dreeves hissed, giving me a shove. "You're on, boy . . . you're on!"

Directly in front of me was an awesome bust, big as a laundry truck and shining fiercely in the moonlight. The gold veneer on the nose and cheeks was pitted and scarred, but the features stood out, massive and untouched, like a Mount Rushmore profile. Pecked out on

140

the base of the marble pedestal was the familiar name J U A R E Z. A somber Indian face, grave and unsmiling, very much like Marta's, only 500 times bigger.

The crowd was hushed and respectful. I slithered along the front row to the next pedestal. Behind me, moving through the throng, excusing himself politely, came Dreeves. "Eight minutes, Navvy!" he hissed. "Eight minutes!"

Smack in front of the middle bust my knees went slack and a column of ice frosted my throat. H I D A L G O, read the name on the pedestal. A noble face, priestly and contemplative, with a high forehead, straight nose, and broad, sensitive mouth—a man who in real life must have possessed great strength and compassion; only he had no beard, not even a mustache—there wasn't a hair on his face, not a tuft or a whisker. His chin was round and smooth as a rock in a swift-flowing river.

"His... beard," I gasped. "Dreeves... Dreeves! Where's his beard? *Where the fuck's his beard?!?!*"

"Carranza!" Dreeves whispered, trying not to startle the worshipful crowd. "Try Carranza!"

There was only five minutes left when I skidded to a halt in front of the head of Venustiano Carranza. I dashed past the guard and up the steps. Carranza had a beard, a curly, golden tangle of stiff, iron hairs that dribbled below his chin. Could Hetty have been wrong? Could she have confused Carranza with Hidalgo? Feverishly, I worked my hands in and out of the folds, searching for the message. "It's not here!" I shouted. "It's not here!"

"*Señor*," the guard said softly: "What are you doing?"

"The nostrils!" Dreeves shouted, over the protests of several crowd members who tried to quiet him. "Try the

141

nostrils!"

Stretching up on my toes, I drove my fists into the rounded cavities but found nothing, only wide, hairless spaces.

"The ears ... the ears!"

I leaped on the pedestal and grabbed hold of the upper lap of Carranza's right ear and pulled myself up till the hole was at eye level.

"*Señor*," the guard said solemnly as he poked me in the ass with the machine gun, "you must come down from there or I will have to shoot you."

I plunged my arm in as far as it would go and grabbed a handful of air. Around on the other side I did the same, Dreeves calling, "Three minutes! Three minutes!" but found nothing, not even a spider web.

"Hidalgo!" Dreeves yelled. "Go back to Hidalgo!"

The soldier tried to shove me away, but I ducked around him and ran over to the bust of Hidalgo and rammed both fists up the nostrils. Nothing. Cursing, I leaped onto the pedestal and punched my right hand deep into his ear. Again nothing. The guard recovered quickly and double-timed over, flicking off the safety on his weapon. Around the other side of the pedestal I searched frantically in Hidalgo's ear for a clue. My foot slipped and I almost fell, but Dreeves, after decking the guard with a blow to the neck, thrust his shoulder under my leg and propped me up. The crowd started roaring in protest.

"Nothing here!" I cried.

"The mouth!" Dreeves shouted, his gray eyebrows flashing like semaphore signals. *"Look-in-his-mouth!"*

There was less than two minutes to spare when I got around in front of the bust. The chin teetered ominously,

142

making it difficult to reach inside the mouth without cracking my hands against the cast-iron lips. With a nimble side-body block that brought a cry of anger from the crowd, Dreeves flattened another guard hustling over to intercept me. Instead of falling back and opening up lanes for the heads to roll through, the crowd pushed up the steps, cursing and shaking their fists. Into the rocking mouth of Miguel Hidalgo I plunged both hands, fingers probing and gripping. Way at the back of the throat my thumb brushed against a roll of paper. With a shout I snatched it out and turned back toward the crowd and flashed a triumphant grin at the camera grinding relentlessly on the park bench. With trembling fingers I unravelled the message—stiff, heavy rice paper, decorated in the upper right-hand corner with an ornate watermark, but otherwise empty... blank. I turned it over—blank also; completely, totally blank.

Betrayed... hopelessly, *wordlessly*... betrayed. A geyser from my heaving stomach spurted against my teeth. With a howl of execration the crowd spilled over the steps. Around the back of the bust I retreated, flapping the blank message like a surrender flag. Inside the pocket of my linen trousers I took the tough, gristly tweeter I had carefully excised from Marta's crotch and inserted it into the abalone whistle. Then, raising the instrument to my lips, I let go with a piercing shriek, far more intense than what Ricky had heard inside the curl of the perfect wave. The crowd shrank back... the busts stopped rocking. With my fingers I squared the whistle against my tongue and taking a deep, *deep* breath let fly again with a prolonged, vindictive screech, at once terrifying and numbing, a cry of relief and anguish, that whipped out over the city like an iron flash and rang off the mountains to the east. A moment later the vibrations peeled the golden skin off the heads, revealing myriad slits and fissures which widened with a crackling roar and shattered into a thousand pieces.

Wails of pity and fear escaped from the crowd. People swarmed over the rubble snatching chunks of shattered iron and trying pathetically to mold them back into the familiar faces that had haunted and hounded them for so long.

"Holy Jesus, boy," Dreeves groaned. "Where'd you ever pick up lung power like that?"

With a scream of vengeance, the mob grabbed up the broken pieces and started hurling them at me. Dreeves went down under the onslaught, flashing the victory sign. Reaching under my tongue, I yanked out the staple and threw it away. Then I stripped off my tunic and vaulted over the wall at the back of the park and started running for the water. In the dazzling moonlight my shadow shot far ahead, beckoning me on. Behind me, a machine gun kicked up spurts of sand. With each panting step my body underwent a speedy transformation. By the time I reached the surf my skin had regained its rubbery gloss, my limbs flattened out, my fingers melded together. Slits opened up on my throat with a sucking cry. Kicking off my *huaraches* and trousers, I plunged into the comforting oily waters. The mob tumbled over the wall in hot pursuit and stampeded across the beach, clamoring for blood. I could still hear their furious cries long after I plunged below the surface and began swimming with swift, powerful strokes out to sea.

144

CHAPTER VII

1.

O*ceanside, Calif.*—(UPS)—An object washed up on the beach yesterday morning was discovered by lifeguard Doug Blotner around 7 A.M.

At first Blotner thought it was a small whale of the pygmy variety, but experts at the Scripps Institute of Oceanography in La Jolla later identified it as a rare type of water mammal, an ancestor of the whale and the porpoise, dating back over a million years.

"This is a real find," declared an Institute spokesperson. "Perhaps the most significant ichthyological discovery of the century. We plan to study the creature carefully to determine its origins and niche in the evolutionary scale, as well as to discover why, after all these millenia, it has persistently refused to develop into an ordinary human form.

"At this time we're not exactly sure whether it is a throwback to an earlier form of life or a creature with recognizable humanoid features that has evolved ahead of the rest of mankind into an entirely new species."

The creature was still alive said the spokesperson, and after immersion in a freshwater tank at the Institute revived considerably. Yesterday afternoon, the creature took some food, and, according to witnesses, made several humanlike sounds uncannily resembling words

145

A bulletin has been issued throughout Southern California requesting anyone with any knowledge of the creature's identity to please contact the Scripps Institute of Oceanography.

2.

A gurgling awakened me. I opened my eyes and stared up through the water. A dark streak hovered over the end of the diving board. Two pairs of wings, arching out like a dragonfly's, fluttered back and forth.

I thrashed around the drain. The gurgling became louder, and I felt the pull of a strong suction as the drain beneath me opened up. I tried to plug it by sitting down, but the suction was too great and the water continued to swirl out. I jammed my hands and feet into the opening, and hunkered over, cursing and shouting in a stream of bubbles, but the water continued to rush down the drain, reducing the level of the pool.

I shrugged and lay back to await the inevitable. When the water sank below the five-foot mark, I looked up again and saw that the figure on the end of the diving board was not a dragonfly after all, but my father. A grin creased his handsome face, and from his hand dangled a cork by a chain which he swung back and forth over my head like a noose.